Written in the Stars

Written in the Stars

Early Stories

Lois Duncan

LIZZIE
SKURNICK
BOOKS

Brooklyn, New York

Printed in the United States
10 9 8 7 6 5 4 3 2 1

No part of this book may be used or reproduced in any manner
without written permission of the publisher.
Please direct inquiries to:
Lizzie Skurnick Books
an imprint of Ig Publishing
392 Clinton Avenue #1S
Brooklyn, NY 11238
www.igpub.com

ISBN: 978-1-939601-14-8 (paperback)
ISBN: 978-1-939601-20-9 (hardcover)
ISBN: 978-1-939601-21-6 (ebook)

For "The Sea Horse Society"—two dozen of my high school classmates who get together each month for lunch and to share the ups and downs of each other's lives. You "girls" are just as important to me today as you were when I wrote these stories.

Contents

Prologue

I often hear from young readers who are working on author reports, and the question they ask most often is "Why do you write?"

It's hard to respond to that question other than to say, "I don't have a reason. It's just what I do."

I cannot remember a time when I didn't consider myself a writer. When I was three years old I was dictating stories to my parents, and as soon as I learned to print, I was setting them on paper. I shared a room with my younger brother, and at night I would lie in bed inventing tales to give him nightmares. I would pretend to be the "Moon Fairy," come to deliver the message that the moon was falling toward the earth.

"And what will happen to *me*?" Billy would ask in his quavering little voice.

"You'll be blown up into the sky," the Moon Fairy would tell him. "By the time you come down the world will be gone, so you'll just keep falling forever."

"With no breakfast?" poor Billy would scream hysterically.

Eventually, our parents had the good sense to put us in separate rooms.

Aside from tormenting Billy, I had few hobbies. A plump, shy little girl, I was a bookworm and a dreamer. I grew up in Sarasota, Florida, and spent a lot of my time playing alone in the woods and on the beaches. I had a secret hideaway in the middle of a bamboo clump. I would bend the bamboo until I could straddle it, and then it would spring up, and I would slide down into the hollow at its heart with green stalks all around me and leaves like lace against my face. I'd hide there and read.

Or I'd ride my bicycle. I would pedal for miles along the beach road with the wind blowing in my face and the sun hot on my hair. There was a special point where I turned the bike off the road and walked it down a little path between the dunes. I parked it there and lay on my back in the sand and listened to the waves crash against the rocks and dreamed up stories.

Then I would go home and write them, pecking them out with two fingers on my mother's manual typewriter. When I was ten I started shipping them off to magazines that I found on my parents' coffee table. Those submissions were quickly returned, and I finally realized that I was choosing the wrong publications. The stories I was writing were about issues that would be of interest only to readers my own age, so I changed my strategy and began to send them to youth publications such as *American Girl, Senior Prom* and *Seventeen*.

At age thirteen, I finally made my first sale. Seeing my byline positioned beneath the title of a story that I had created was one of the most incredible experiences of my life.

From that point on there was no turning back. Or, perhaps, there had never been a time when I could turn back.

For me, a life as a writer was "written in the stars."

Written in
the Stars

Written in the Stars

Ever since I was very little, I knew that someday my prince would come. At first I used to envision him riding up on a snow-white horse to scoop me up and carry me away to his castle. This changed, of course, as I grew older and my reading matter progressed from *Grimm's Fairy Tales* to *Romeo and Juliet*. I did away with the horse by the time I was eleven, but the rest of the belief remained, a quiet certainty deep inside of me. Somewhere in the world there was The One, the special One, looking for me just as I was looking for him, and someday he would come. It was written in the stars.

I never talked about it much, except once in a while to Mother. I dated just as the other girls did, strings of silly, uninteresting boys, just to kill time until The One arrived. And then, when I was seventeen, two things happened. Mother gave me the locket, and I realized who The One was. Ted Bennington.

When I opened the little white package on my seventeenth birthday and saw the locket, I was flabbergasted. The locket was not a new purchase; I had seen it often before. In fact, every time I rummaged through Mother's jewelry box to borrow a pair of earrings or a bracelet or something, I saw it, not in the jumble of everyday jewelry but in the separate little tray where she kept all the things Daddy had given her. There was the whole story of a romance in that tray—Daddy's track medals from college and his fraternity pin, the pearls he gave Mother on their wedding day and the silver pin from their fifteenth anniversary and the silver bars he wore when he was in the Navy during the war. And in the midst of all those things was the locket.

"But, Mother," I protested, holding it up in amazement, "you can't really mean for me to have this! It's yours! It belongs to you!"

"Indeed I do," Mother said decidedly. "It represents a lot to me, honey. I've always said that my daughter would have it when she turned seventeen." There was a faraway look in her eyes.

"But why seventeen?" I asked. "That's hardly a milestone like sweet sixteen or eighteen or twenty-one. Seventeen really isn't anything."

"It was to me," Mother said. "It was the age of heartbreak."

I stared at her in disbelief. "Your heart was never broken!"

It was impossible to imagine Daddy, with his warm gray eyes and gentle smile, ever breaking anyone's heart, least of all Mother's. Mother and Daddy had one of the best marriages I had ever known. They always seemed to have fun together, no matter where they were or what they were doing. And they loved each other. You could tell it just by being around them. It wasn't the grabbing, hanging onto sort of love that kids our age experienced, it went deeper; it was the sort of love that made Mother say two years ago when Daddy died, "Well, I've had more happiness in my eighteen years of marriage than most women have in fifty."

"Oh, it was broken, all right," Mother said lightly. "And yours will be too, dear. It's inevitable." Then she kissed me.

I laughed, a little embarrassed, because we're not usually a very demonstrative family. Besides, I wasn't quite sure what Mother was talking about. But I did love the locket. It was tiny and heart-shaped on a thin gold chain, and it was delicate and old-fashioned and lovely. I felt about it the way Mother did about her engagement ring—"Much too valuable just to wear around." I wrapped it in tissue paper and put it in the corner of my top bureau drawer.

The locket wasn't the only present I received on my seventeenth birthday. Besides that, Mother gave me an evening dress, ankle length, dark rose taffeta, and Nancy, my best friend, gave me the rose slippers to wear with it. But the gift that topped everything, that caused my stomach to lurch and my heart to beat faster, was a simple blue scarf with a gold border. It came from Ted Bennington.

"I hope you like it," he said awkwardly. "I didn't know. I haven't had much experience picking things out for girls."

"I love it," I assured him. "It's just beautiful."

I suppressed a desire to lean over and kiss him. It would have been so easy to do because I liked him so much. I liked the way his blond, curly hair fell forward over his forehead, and his honest blue eyes and nice square chin. And I liked his being shy and sweet and serious and a little awkward; it was so different from the smooth know-it-alls in our senior class. I thought, I would like to kiss you, Ted Bennington. But I didn't say it. And I didn't kiss him.

Instead I reached over and squeezed his hand and smiled at him and said, "It's beautiful," again. Which must have been the right thing to do, because he squeezed my hand and smiled back at me.

I had begun dating Ted a couple of months before that. It was funny how it started. Ted must have been in my class for years and years, and I never really noticed him. In fact, nobody noticed him. He was a quiet boy and he wasn't on any of the teams or in the student government or in any of the clubs; he worked after school and on weekends in Parks Drug Store. I think that might have been one of the things that made him shy, having to work when the other kids goofed around. "It made me feel funny," he told me later, "having to serve Cokes and malts and things to the kids and then seeing them in school the next day. You can't actually be buddies with people who leave you ten-cent tips."

"But none of the other kids felt like that," I told him. "They never gave it a moment's thought. They would have been glad to be friends anytime if you'd acted like you wanted to."

"I know that now," Ted said. "But it took you to show me."

Which was true. It was cold-blooded in a way. I didn't have a date to the Homecoming Dance and was on the lookout for someone to take me. You don't have too much choice when you're a senior and most of the senior boys are going steady with juniors and sophomores. So I made a mental list of the boys who were left and crossed off the ones who were too short, and that left four. Ronny Brice weighs three hundred pounds, and Steven Porter can't stand me, and Stanley Pierce spits when he talks. Which left Ted.

"Do you know if Ted Bennington's asked anyone to Homecoming?" I asked Nancy.

Nancy gave me a surprised look. "Who?"

"Ted Bennington," I said. "The blond boy in our English class. The quiet one."

"Oh," Nancy said. "I didn't know that was his name. No, I don't suppose he has. He doesn't date, does he? I've never seen him at any of the dances."

"No," I said. "I suppose he doesn't. But there's always a first time."

The next morning I got to English class early and as Ted came in I gave him a real once-over. I was surprised. There was nothing wrong with his looks. He wasn't awfully tall, but he had a nice build and good features and an honest, clean-cut look about him. I even liked the back of his neck.

Ted Bennington, I thought, you may not know it now, but you are going to take me to the Homecoming Dance.

And I managed it. It is a little shameful to me now to think about how calculating I was—a smile here, a sideways look there, "Hi, Ted," ever time I passed him in the hall. "Which chapters did she say we were to read tonight, Ted?" as we left class and happened to reach the door together. A week or two of that and then the big step. "Nancy's having a party this weekend, Ted. A girl-ask-boy affair. Would you like to go?" It was really pretty easy.

Ted was standing at his locker when I asked him. He had the locker door open and was fishing out his gym shorts, and when he turned he looked surprised, as though he wasn't sure he had heard me correctly.

"Go? You mean, with you?"

"Yes."

"Why—why, sure. Thanks. I'd like to." He looked

terribly pleased and a little embarrassed, as if he had never taken a girl anywhere in his entire life.

"What night is the party?" he asked now. "And what time? And where do you live?"

We stood there a few minutes, exchanging the routine information, and I began to wonder if maybe I was making a mistake asking Ted to the party, to that particular party anyway, because it would be The Crowd, the school leaders, the group I had run around with since kindergarten days. And Ted wasn't one of them.

But it was too late then to uninvite him, so I let it go, trying not to worry too much as the week drew to a close, and on Saturday night at eight sharp Ted arrived at my house.

He made a good impression on Mother. I could see that right away. He had that air of formal politeness that parents like. When we left, Mother said, "Have fun, kids," and didn't ask, "What time will the party be over?" which is how I always could tell whether she approved of my dates.

Ted didn't have a car, so we walked to Nancy's, and it was a nice walk. Everything went off well at the party too. The Crowd seemed surprised to see Ted at first, but they accepted him more easily than I had thought possible. Ted relaxed after the first few minutes and made a real effort to fit in; he danced and took part in the games and talked to people.

Even Nancy was surprised.

"You know," she said when we were out in the kitchen together getting the soft drinks out of the refrigerator, "that Ted Bennington—he's really a very nice guy. How come we've overlooked him before this?"

I said, "I don't know." I was wondering the same thing.

I wondered it even more as we walked home afterward, talking about the party and school and what we were going to do after we graduated, comfortable talk as if we'd known each other forever. I told Ted I was going to secretarial school, and he told me he was working toward a scholarship to Tulane where he wanted to study medicine. I learned that his mother was a widow, as mine was, and that he had three sisters, and that he played the guitar. The moonlight slanted down through the branches of the trees that lined the street, making splotches of light and shadow along the sidewalk, and the air was crisp with autumn, and I was very conscious of my hand, small and empty, swinging along beside me. His hand was swinging too, and after a while they sort of bumped into each other. We walked the rest of the way without saying much, just holding hands and walking through the patches of moonlight.

The next morning Nancy phoned to ask if Ted had invited me to Homecoming.

"To Homecoming? Why, no," I said. And to my amazement I realized that I had completely forgotten about Homecoming—that, now, somehow, it didn't matter very much.

When the time came, of course, we did go, but, now that I think back on it, I don't think Ted ever did actually ask me. We just went, quite naturally, because by then we went everywhere together.

When did I realize that he was The One? I'm trying hard to remember. I guess there was no special time that the realization came. It just grew, a quiet knowledge deep inside me. It grew out of our walks together, long hikes through the autumn woods with the trees blowing wild and red and gold against the deep blue of the sky, and the winter picnics with The Crowd, sitting on blankets around a fire with snow piled behind us and Ted's arm around my shoulders. He brought his guitar sometimes to those, and we all sang.

"Why didn't you tell us you played the guitar?" somebody asked him, and Ted grinned sheepishly and said, "I didn't know that anybody would be interested."

It grew, the realization, through the long lovely spring days and easy talk and laughter and a feeling of companionship I had never known before with any boy or, for that matter, with any girl, even Nancy. One Sunday evening (we had been to church together that morning and to the beach all afternoon and to an early movie after dinner), Ted said, "We fit so well together, you and I," and I said, "Yes," and Ted said, "It's as if it were meant to be that way."

"You mean," I said, and the words came haltingly to my tongue because I had never said them aloud to him before and I was afraid they would sound silly, "You mean, as though it were written in the stars?"

Ted was silent a moment and then he said, "Yes, I guess that's what I mean."

It was the night of the Senior Prom that Ted saw the locket. As I said before, I didn't wear it often, it was too precious, but somehow the night of the Senior Prom seemed right. I wore my rose evening dress and my rose slippers and no jewelry except the locket on its slender gold chain.

Ted noticed it right away.

"Nice," he commented. "Makes you look sort of sweet and old-fashioned. Is it a family heirloom?"

"You could say that," I said. "Daddy gave it to Mother, and Mother gave it to me." I touched it fondly.

Ted was interested. "Does it open?"

"I don't know," I said.

"Let's see." He reached over and took the locket in his hands, the gentle, capable hands I had grown to know so well, and fiddled with it for a moment, and it fell open on his palm, disclosing a tiny lock of hair.

"So!" he said, smiling. "I didn't know your father had red hair."

"I guess he must have when he was young. He got gray very early." I smiled too. "Put it back, Ted. It belongs there."

He did so, closing the locket gently as though anything that had meaning for me had meaning for him also.

I'd tell you about the summer, but it is too hard to describe. I think you must already know what it's like to be in love. You get up in the morning and shower and dress and eat breakfast just as you always have, but ever motion, every ordinary thing, is flavored with excitement. "I'm going to see him today—in two hours—one hour—ten minutes—and now he is here!"—there's a radiance, a silent singing inside you that seems to expand to fill your life. That was the summer—and then, so terribly soon, it was autumn again.

Ted got his scholarship. His face, when he told me, was shining with excitement.

"How do you like the sound of it—*Doctor* Bennington!"

"Wonderful," I said. "Marvelous! But I'll miss you."

"I'll miss you too." He sobered. "I'll be home on vacations."

"Sure," I said. The summer lay golden and glorious behind us; there would be other summers.

"I wish—" His voice trembled slightly. "I wish you were going to Tulane too."

"I'll be here for you to come back to," I said. "I'll be a secretary in a year, you know. Maybe I can come there and get a job that has some connection with the college."

"That would be great." Still he did not smile. "I'm afraid," he said suddenly.

"Afraid of what?"

"Of going. Of leaving you here. I'm afraid something will happen, that you'll meet somebody else or something. What we've got—it's so right—so perfect! We can't lose it!"

"We won't," I said with confidence. You don't lose something that is written in the stars.

And so my prince rode away on his snow-white horse, and that was the beginning of the end. We did not marry. If we had, I wouldn't bother telling this story. Ted went to college and I to secretarial school, and we wrote letters at first constantly, and then not quite so often. Ted couldn't afford to come home at Thanksgiving, and when he did come at Christmas I had the measles, (horrible thing to have when you're practically grown), and we did not really get to see each other until spring vacation. By then we had been so long apart that we spent the whole vacation getting re-acquainted, and then it was time for Ted to go back again. He was as sweet and wonderful as ever, you understand; we just felt as though we didn't know each other quite so well.

"Don't forget me," he said a little desperately as he left.

And I said, "Of course not," but this time I did not sound so certain.

As it turned out, it was Ted who met somebody else; he who had been so worried, when I had been so sure! But in the end it was Ted who wrote the letter. The girl, he said, was a premed student just as he was. Her name—well, I've forgotten her name—but she was small, he said, and had hazel eyes and was smart and fun and easy to talk to. I would like her, he said. We were alike in many ways. He said he was sorry.

It was raining the day the letter came. I read it in the living room and then gave it to Mother to read and went upstairs to my room.

I lay on the bed and listened to the sound of the rain and thought how strange it was, how unbelievable. I didn't hate Ted; you don't hate somebody as sweet as Ted. I didn't even hate the girl. I was too numb to feel anything; I didn't even cry. I just lay there listening to the rain and thinking, he was The One—we were right—we fitted—we were perfect. Now he is gone and he was The One, and he will never come again.

I was still lying there when Mother came in. She did not knock, she just opened the door and came in and stood by the bed looking down at me. Before she said it, I knew what she was going to say.

"There will be other boys," she said. "You may not believe it now, but there will be."

"Yes," I replied. "I suppose so." There was no use arguing about something like that. "Ted was The One," I said. "There will be other boys, sure, but he was The One."

Mother was silent a moment. Then she said, "Do you still have the locket?"

"The locket?" I was surprised at the question. "Yes, of course. It's in my top drawer."

Mother went over to the bureau and opened the drawer. She took out the locket and brought it over to the bed.

"Put it on," she said.

"Now?" I was more surprised. "But, why? Why now?"

"Because," Mother said quietly, "this is why I gave it to you." She put the locket in my hands and sat down on the edge of the bed, watching me as I raised it and put the chain around my neck and fumbled the tiny clasp into place. "You see," she said when I had finished, "that locket was given to *me* by The One on the evening of our engagement. We were very young, and he couldn't afford a ring yet. The locket had been in his family for a very long time."

"Oh." I reached up and touched the locket, feeling a new reverence for it. I thought of Daddy drawing it from his pocket, nervous, excited, watching Mother's face as he did so, hoping desperately that she would like it. Mother and Daddy—young and newly in love, two people I had never known and would never know.

"He was everything," Mother continued, "that I ever wanted in a husband. He was good and strong and honest, he was tender, he was fun to be with, and he loved me with all his heart. He was without doubt written for me in the stars." She paused and then said, "He was killed in a train wreck three weeks later."

"He what!" I regarded her with bewilderment. "But you said—I thought—" I realized suddenly what she was telling me. "You mean it wasn't Daddy? You loved somebody before Daddy, somebody you thought was The One, and then—"

"I didn't just think it," Mother interrupted. "If I had married him I'm sure I would have been a happy woman and loved *him* all my life. As it worked out, three years later I married your father, and I have been a happy woman and loved him all my life. What I am trying to tell you, honey"—she leaned forward, searching for just the right words—"There is no One. There are men and there are women. There are many fine men who can give you love and happiness. Ted was probably one of those, but Ted came into your life too soon."

"But," I protested weakly, "that's so cold-blooded, so sort of—of—" I felt as though I were losing the prince on the snow-white horse, the dream that was bright with the wonder of childhood.

"I'm saying," Mother said gently, "that there are many men worthy of loving. And the one of those who comes along *at the right time*—*he* is the One who is written for you in the stars."

She went out then and closed the door and left me alone, listening to the rain and fingering the locket. I stared at the door that Mother had just closed behind her.

And then I began thinking of the other door, the one she had just opened.

(written at the age of 20)

I was married two days after my nineteenth birthday, at the end of my freshman year of college. During that year I had fallen in love with a senior, who now was graduating and joining the Air Force. I was frightened that being apart might mean the end of our relationship, so when he proposed, I said yes.

It was an unwise marriage and lasted only nine years.

I wrote this story one year after our wedding, at a time

when I still was telling myself I was happy.

When writing it, I drew upon fragments of past experiences: my gentle romance with a sweet, shy boy in high school; a story my mother had told me about her first fiancé who was killed in a train wreck; an experience one of my friends had had when she and her high school boyfriend attended different colleges.

That was all this story was supposed to be.

When I read it now, however, I find something in it that I do not think I meant to put there. Was it possible that already I was starting to question, without allowing myself to realize it, the rightness of that step I had taken so hastily? If I had waited until I was wiser, more experienced, more mature, might I have chosen differently?

Was this handsome young man, with whom I was starting to discover I had little in common, truly The One who was written for me in the stars?

Return

The curtains were crisp and ruffled at the windows. Outside it was still not quite dark, still just on the edge of twilight when fireflies were beginning to twinkle in the hedge by the walk.

Inside, the kitchen was warm and bright, and the biscuits were baked a little too long, and the woman was smiling across the table while the little boy was feeding a chicken wing to the cat.

Bill looked at them and thought, Well, I'm here.

He thought it in an odd, detached way, as though he were not really there at all.

Last night on the train he had buried his face in the hard Pullman pillow and thought, Just seventeen more hours! Just seventeen more hours and I'll be home! He had seen himself crossing the yard, opening the front door, going into the hall; he had smelled the cedar wood chest and heard the tick of the hall clock. Then he had gone through the living room into the kitchen, and they had all been there—the woman and the little boy and a serious man with graying hair—and they had hugged each other and laughed and eaten supper together in the kitchen with the twilight outside.

Last night he had been terribly excited.

Now he was here, and he was not excited at all.

"What's the matter, dear?" asked his mother anxiously. "Are the biscuits too brown for you?"

"No," Bill said quickly. "Of course not. They're just the way I like them."

"You're not eating very much, dear."

"Yes, I am," Bill said. "You just haven't been noticing."

He helped himself to another biscuit and buttered it industriously.

"Do they feed you biscuits in the army, Billy?" the little boy asked with interest.

"Sure, Jerry, but not like these."

"I remembered how you always liked biscuits," said his mother, "so the first thing I thought when we got your telegram was how we could have biscuits for supper when you got home. Remember how you and your father used to eat two whole plates of biscuits at one meal?"

"Yes," said Bill, and then he said, "It seems odd without Dad."

"Yes," said his mother. "It does."

The light went out of her eyes, but she still smiled, a determined smile.

"I—I didn't get your letter about the accident until six weeks after it happened," Bill went on awkwardly. "We were behind enemy lines and weren't getting any mail. I wrote as soon as I heard."

"Yes, dear. I'm sure you did."

"I guess maybe I didn't sound like I wanted to. I don't write very good letters."

"It was all right, Bill," his mother said. "I understood."

Bill nodded gratefully, but he knew she had not understood, because he had not fully understood himself. There had been a stack of letters at one time, ten from his mother and sixteen from Mary. He had read Mary's first—*Dearest Bill*—chitchat about college, the last football game, Arden and Mike going steady—*I miss you so much. All my love, Mary*. He had read slowly and pictured her as she wrote, her face flushed and pretty, her pen racing along the page as she spilled out her thoughts helter-skelter before they had time to get away. When he had finished, he started his mother's letters—accounts of the Garden Club, Jerry's toothache, a new paint job on the car—and finally, the accident.

The letter about the accident had been heart-breaking and brief.

Bill had read it carefully and laid it aside. He had thought, My father is dead, but he had not felt any great sorrow, only numbed disbelief.

That night he had dreamed about rows and rows of men, all dead, but none of them was like his father. They were young men with drawn yellow faces; and suddenly they weren't dead at all, but twisting and turning and screaming in horrible fits of agony. The dream was so real that he awoke with a scream ringing in his ears.

He had lain very still in his blankets and thought, My father is dead. But he could not believe it was true. Death was something close and horrible and frantic, something his gentle, easygoing father could know nothing about.

He had groped for his flashlight and, when he had found it, he had read Mary's letters again. *I miss you so much. All my love, Mary.*

When he had gone to sleep that time, he had not dreamed again.

Bill jumped as the cat wound itself around his leg.

"New cat, isn't it?" he asked.

His mother said, "A female cat came along, and Tuffy went away with her. This is Pepper."

Jerry leaned forward in his seat, a small, pale boy with glasses.

"Billy," he said eagerly, "did you ever kill anybody?"

After a moment Bill said, "Yes."

"With a gun?"

"No," said Bill. "With a bayonet."

His stomach contracted and the chicken tasted like meal.

His mother said, "Jerry, you may excuse yourself and go upstairs to your room. I'll be up to talk to you in a few minutes."

Bill felt the bayonet, warm and strong in his hands. He felt it pressed against him as he ran. He saw a man in front of him, and he watched the end of the bayonet, and he saw the man's face when they met—

"Oh, Mother," Jerry protested, "why? Why do I have to go up now? It's not even half-past eight yet!"

Bill got up quickly.

"I have to go," he said. "I've got a date."

"But, Bill, you haven't had your dessert yet!"

Bill said, "Save it for me and I'll eat it later. When I talked to Mary on the phone I told her I'd be by at eight-thirty."

He went outside. It was really dark now, and the fireflies were fairy lanterns across the lawn.

Bill stood in the darkness and breathed deeply and the sickness went away. Then he got into the car and drove to Mary's.

Her father came to the door. He was much smaller than Bill remembered him.

"Well," he exclaimed, "look who's here! How are you, Bill?"

Bill said, "It's good to see you."

They shook hands. Mary's mother came in from the kitchen with the two sisters, the one who played the piano and the little one with the braces, only she wasn't little now and the braces were gone.

Mary came in.

She was plumper than Bill remembered, and her hair was cut short and fluffy around her face instead of long over her shoulders, but she was still Mary.

She said, "Hi, there, Bill."

"Hello, Mary."

Then in the car, she was close and warm beside him.

"Where do you want to go?" he asked.

"There's a party over at Angie's. We might go there." She hesitated. "Or we could go to a movie?"

Bill said, "Let's skip the party. I'd kind of like to have you to myself this evening."

Mary said, "All right. I think it will be a stupid party anyway, and the movie's a good one."

The movie was terrible. Bill sat stiffly in the cramped seat, conscious of Mary's presence beside him. He could smell her perfume and feel the warmth of her shoulder pressed against his. Finally he stopped all pretense of watching the screen and shifted his full gaze to her and saw that she was crying because the woman in the movie could not make up her mind between the two men.

Bill felt embarrassed. He had forgotten how Mary cried in movies. Before he had always teased her about it and found it strangely touching. Now, suddenly, it was ridiculous.

"Come on, Mary," he said, "let's go."

"This isn't where we came in!"

"We'll see it some other time."

He got up and made his way between the sets to the exit. Mary followed him, pouting.

"Bill, I don't understand what's the matter with you."

"I don't know either," he said apologetically. "I'm sorry. The movie was getting on my nerves, and I wanted to go somewhere quiet where I could just sit and talk to you for a while. I guess I can stand the rest of it, though, if you want to go back in."

Mary sighed.

"No," she said. "Let's do what you want to do tonight."

They got into the car.

He said, "Tonight's the first time I've driven a car for six months."

"What was the last time?"

"It was a Jeep, and I didn't drive it very far."

He drove out along the river road to their old parking place by the water, but when he reached it there were two cars already there. He swore a little under his breath and stepped on the gas.

A side road loomed up on his left. He slowed down, turned the car into it and stopped.

The wind came up from the river and breathed through

the car windows, soft and cool.

"Thanks for writing so much," Bill said at last to break the silence.

Mary said, "You hardly wrote at all."

"I know. I didn't have time."

"I didn't either," Mary said. "It's hard to do all the things you really have to do in college, much less write letters. But I *made* time for that."

"It was swell," Bill said. His voice was strained.

What's the matter with me? he asked himself angrily. I've been away two years, and now I'm with my girl and there's nothing to say!

Always before there had been too much to say, things that would not go into letters when he sat down to write them. He would get as far as *Dear Mary,* and the paper would stare up at him, white and empty, and the things he wanted to tell her would not be written down. Instead he would say, *There have been some men sick,* but never how they looked with the sickness and how they smelled and how he felt when he saw them; or, *A man was shot yesterday,* but never a description of a man with half of his face missing, a man who used to chew gum and play a guitar. He did not write, *I'm lonely. I'm sick. I'm scared.* Those were things he whispered to Mary in the secret night and saved to tell Mary when he got home and they were together.

Now he took a deep breath.

"Mary," he said, "I killed a man."

He waited for her to shiver, to gasp, to be horrified. He waited for the tears that came so easily at a movie.

Instead she said, "I guess everybody did, didn't they?"

"I don't know," Bill said. "I guess they did."

He wanted her to share the horror of it, and in that way perhaps the horror would go away.

"After all," Mary said, "that's what you were there for, to protect our country."

"But he was a man," Bill said, "and I killed him. He was a live man, and now he isn't alive."

He shuddered and the old familiar sickness went through him.

"Bill," Mary said suddenly, "have you met another girl?"

"What?"

"I said, is there another girl?"

For a moment Bill was sure that she was joking, but then he realized that he was not.

"No," he said. "There's no other girl. How on earth could I have met another girl?"

"I don't know," she said. "It's just that you're acting so odd. I thought maybe you had met someone else."

"No," Bill said again. "There's nobody but you."

He put his arms around her and pulled her to him and kissed her. When he kissed her the strain went away and the years between them were gone; it was the night of the Senior Prom, and he was very young and in love. He lifted his face and pressed it against her hair, and for a moment he was filled with peace. He was home and everything was all right.

"Mary," he whispered, "oh, honey, I missed you so!"

"I missed you too, Bill."

"Mary," he said, "let's get married. Let's get married now."

He could feel her start.

"Get married?"

"We'd have the rest of this leave together before I have to go back. Please, Mary!"

She pulled away from him and looked at his serious face.

"Bill," she said nervously, "Don't be silly. I couldn't stop college and get married now. Daddy would have a fit if I even suggested such a thing. And what good would it do? You'd be away all the time."

Bill released her and leaned back against the seat.

"Yes," he said wearily, "of course, you're right. It would be a nutty thing to do. It's just that you'd belong to me then, and I'd belong to you. Right now I don't feel like I belong anywhere. Everything's so different from when I left."

"I'm not different," Mary said.

"Yes, you are. We used to not even have to talk, we understood each other so well. Now it's like we didn't know each other at all."

"You do have another girl," Mary said miserably. "I can tell."

This time Bill did not try to deny it. He started the motor.

"It's getting late," he said. "I'd better take you home."

When they reached the house Mary opened the car door and started across the lawn.

"It's all right," she said, "I can walk to the door by myself."

"Mary!" Bill caught her.

She stopped and turned back to him; there was no anger in her face, only unhappiness.

"Mary, there isn't any girl!"

Mary said, "I know there isn't any other girl. I almost wish there were. At least then we'd know what was wrong!"

Bill stood in the yard and watched the hall light go off and later a light go on upstairs. Then he got back into the car. He started it and pressed the accelerator to the floor and watched the needle creep up across the speedometer. He drove out along the river road again, faster and faster until the sound of the wind past the window was a dull roar. He had driven like this once before, in a Jeep, but suddenly the road had ended and the Jeep had gone off into the underbrush where a man was sleeping. Bill and the man had stared into each other faces, and the man had groped in the bush beside him for his gun, and Bill had picked up his bayonet ...

Bill slowed down and drove quietly back to town. He drove home, because there was no place else to go.

He crossed the yard and went up the porch steps and opened the door. It was like going into a stranger's house, a house that was oddly familiar as from a dream, but not a place where he himself had lived. In his mind were other houses, tumbled masses of houses without walls and without roofs and with all their life gone from them. He stepped into the hall and closed the door behind him, but he could not shut the ghost houses out.

The light was on in the living room. His mother looked up when he came in.

"There's a piece of cake for you in the kitchen."

He hesitated.

"Were you waiting up for me?"

"Yes," his mother said. "I know it's silly, but I couldn't

sleep until I knew you were in."

Bill thought, how old she looks! Why, Dad and I always used to think she was the prettiest lady in town!

"It hasn't been easy with Dad gone, has it, Mom?"

It did not sound the way he had meant it to sound.

She said, "No, dear, it hasn't been easy. But we're getting along."

He wanted to go to her and put his arms around her in a protective gesture, the way his father would have, the way he himself would have so short a time ago. He wanted to say, "Oh, Mother, I'm glad to be back!" He wanted to hug her and say, "Mother, you're still the prettiest lady in town!" But the shadows of the past two years were all about him, close and real and a part of him.

He looked at his mother, and they could not reach each other.

He said, "Mom, have I changed so very much?"

"It's the war, Bill," she said slowly, carefully. "War makes boys grow up too fast. It turns them into men before they are ready and teaches them things they should never know."

"But why?" he demanded unreasonably. "Why? What's the matter with me? What in God's name has happened to me?"

His mother was startled by his outburst.

"Don't look that way, Bill! Everything will be all right, dear. Just give it time and everything will be all right."

He hadn't cried much when he was a child. Now, when he cried, it was the way a man cries when he is lost and afraid.

"Mother," he sobbed, "oh, Mother, I want to come home!"

She went to him and put her arms around him the way one comforts a child. But he was no longer a child.

"There, there, son," she said helplessly. "You *are* home."

She went out to the kitchen to get his piece of cake.

(written at the age of 18)

First Place Winner in *Seventeen Magazine's* Creative Writing Contest, 1953

☆ ☆ ☆ ☆ ☆ ☆ ☆ ☆ ☆ ☆ ☆ ☆ ☆ ☆

What was it about this story that caused it to win a national award?

I wish I knew. I have a feeling there was some reason other than the quality of the writing. Perhaps it stood out from the competition because of the male viewpoint and therefore got an especially careful reading. Perhaps one of the judges had a son in the service. Perhaps the story seemed more important because it was about war and death instead of proms and parties.

Perhaps it was the ending. The ending doesn't follow the rules of plotting that most youth publications of that day adhered to. It differed from "Written in the Stars" in that I did not have an all-wise mother solve the problem, because the problem is unsolvable. The mother's pathetic token gesture of bringing in a piece of cake is symbolic of the futility of any loving woman's efforts to undo the emotional damage done to her son by war. If this story had been submitted by an adult writer, I doubt that *Seventeen* would have bought and published it. They would have thought it too depressing for their vulnerable young readers. The fact that it was one of those vulnerable readers who wrote the story altered the situation.

I named the young man in the story Bill, not because it was my brother's name (which it was), but because it was solid, down-to-earth and all-American. The Bill in the story had no personality quirks to set him apart from the rest of humanity.

He was Every Man.

The Wish

Jane slumped on her bed. "Oh," she moaned, "why did I ever say I would go!"

Downstairs she could hear the clatter of supper dishes being washed, her father's radio, her mother and Alice laughing together in the kitchen.

Jane had told them at dinner. Alice had said, "I think I'm going to take a night off and get to bed early for a change," and their mother had answered, "Good for you, dear; you've been out too many nights this week as it is." Their father had nodded.

Jane had said, "I have a date tonight."

There was a moment of silence. Everyone stared at her in surprise.

"It's with a boy named Kent," Jane continued matter-of-factly. "Kent Browning." She was pleased with herself for the way she said it, calmly, casually, as though she had dates every night, as though it were nothing to become excited about at all.

"Kent Browning," Alice repeated. "I don't believe I know him. Is he in your class?" Now that Alice was in college, she no longer knew all the high school boys.

"No," Jane said, "he's here for the summer. He's visiting Ed Morris."

Her mother found her voice at last. "Why, that's lovely, dear. Where are you going?"

"To the Country Club dance. We're doubling with Ed and Kathy."

The family was still staring at her, dumfounded, when she excused herself to get ready. "Is it all right if I don't help with the dishes tonight?"

"Of course!" Her mother rose too. "Can I help you, dear? Is your dress pressed? Do you have a good pair of nylons?"

"What's he like, Jane? Is he nice?" Alice asked.

"I don't know," Jane said. "I've never met him. Kathy set up the date."

Suddenly the miracle was gone. Her family melted from amazement into understanding. No boy had asked Jane for a date—Kathy had been the one to arrange it. Kathy called herself Ed's girl, but half the boys in school were enthralled with her, and she encouraged them all. Whenever Ed asked her to get one of his friends a date, Kathy blithely skipped over her own group of friends and chose someone who supplied no competition—usually Jane.

"Oh." Alice got up and started toward the kitchen. "Well, you can take my new evening bag if you like."

"Thanks." Jane went slowly upstairs. The date was no longer a bright, shining opportunity; it was only an evening and would go as flat as any other date evening. The boy would arrive, and he would be good-looking, because all Ed's friends were good-looking: he would look at Jane and try not to appear too disappointed, and they would get into the car with Ed and Kathy, and Kathy would be beautiful. The evening would pass, somehow, and finally Jane would be home again and the date would be over.

In a wave of hopelessness, Jane took her strapless evening gown off its hanger and hauled it unceremoniously over her head. Then she sat down in front of the dressing table to put on her lipstick.

All she could see in the face that looked out at her from the mirror were freckles and a tight-lipped mouth, full of braces. "It's your fault," Jane told the face furiously. "Why can't you look like Alice?" It was hard to have a pretty sister, especially when that sister looked so very much like yourself. Feature by feature, Jane was forced to admit that she and Alice were practically identical, and yet not a soul hesitated to call Alice pretty.

"It's not fair," Jane said bitterly. She got up in despair and crossed to the window. The sky was deep and the stars were bright and very near the earth.

Jane chose one, almost without thinking, and said, "Star light, star bright—first star I've seen tonight." The childish words of the old rhyme were familiar and reassuring. How many thousands of times had she wished on stars! First with Alice, and then, when Alice grew older, by herself—always the same wish, but it had never come true.

"I wish," Jane said softly, "that I were beautiful."

The stars seemed to lean nearer the earth, as though to hear her better, and Jane heard her words ringing soft and clear through the night: *"I—wish—that—I—were—beautiful."* The night flowed in through the open window, close and warm and filled with magic. *"Beautiful!"* it echoed. *"I—were—beautiful."* Jane caught her breath.

What would it feel like to be beautiful? How would it feel if, when she looked in the mirror, the familiar freckled face was gone and in its place there was one she had never seen before? It would be lovely, with deep violet eyes, a flawless complexion, white, even teeth. A glow swept over her and she stood there, feeling beauty spreading over her, hardly daring to breathe.

She sat down weakly on the foot of her bed. "I know," she whispered. "I know how it feels to be beautiful! That must have been the right star!"

Downstairs the doorbell rang. There was a rattle of newspapers as her father got up to answer it—the sound of the door opening—voices.

"Jane!" Her father's voice. "Your friends are here."

"Jane!" Her father called again.

"Coming!" Jane hesitated, and then turned toward the door. "I won't look," she told herself softly. "I feel beautiful. If I look, I might break the spell!"

Instead, she threw open the top bureau drawer and rummaged quickly through it until she found Alice's evening bag, hurriedly transferred her lipstick and comb, and started for the stairs.

Kent was standing in the living room with her father. He was a tall, blond boy with broad shoulders and an easy smile. He smiled now as he saw Jane.

"Hello." He stepped forward to meet her. "I guess you're Jane. I'm Kent Browning."

Jane felt herself begin to freeze, the way she always did when she had to meet new people. She began to draw her lips tightly together to conceal the braces, and then suddenly remembered. Any boy in the world should be glad to go out with a beautiful girl! The thought was such a new one for her that she smiled despite herself.

"Hello, Kent," she said warmly, taking the hand he

offered. "I'm glad to meet you." She glanced sideways at her father's startled face. "I see you've met my dad."

"Yes—sure." Kent's eyes didn't leave her face.

"Well, we'd better not keep Ed and Kathy waiting. Good night, Daddy. We won't be late."

Kent had the door open, and a moment later they were outside, walking toward Ed's car.

"Here we are," Kent said, opening the back door and helping Jane in.

"Hi, Jane!" Ed said as he started the car, "How are you doing?"

"Fine, thanks, Ed. Hi, Kathy."

Kathy turned in the front seat, tossed casually over her shoulder, "Hello, Jane. Sorry we're late. I held things up by taking too long getting dressed. Aren't I terrible?"

"Horrible," Jane agreed pleasantly, "but we'll forgive her, won't we, Kent?"

She heard her own voice, light and teasing and sure of itself. Just the way she had always wanted it to sound. Always before, when she had tried to sound careless and gay, the words stuck in her throat and came out in jerky, self-conscious lumps, but now suddenly it was easy. How could anyone be self-conscious when she felt beautiful?

"Maybe you can forgive her," Kent said, "but I can't. It's made our evening fifteen minutes shorter." He laughed, and Jane laughed with him, liking the warmth in his voice.

Kathy turned to them in obvious surprise. "Hey," she said, "is this a budding romance?"

Ed said, "You'd better watch that guy, Janie."

Jane had never been to the Country Club before. She had sometimes passed it at night, driving home from a movie with her family, and heard the music and laughter swelling out into the night. She had daydreamed about it—imagined herself stepping through the door into the fairyland of gaiety within—but the dreams had been tinged with a kind of terror. "What would I do if I were there?" She had imagined herself standing awkwardly in the middle of the dance floor, staring into the unhappy face of her escort, while dozens of glamorous, graceful couples whirled by. But tonight was different. Tonight was a magical night.

When they stepped into the ballroom, Jane gave a little gasp of delight. "Why, it's beautiful!" she exclaimed. "Just the way I imagined it would be!"

"You mean you haven't been here before?" Kent was amazed.

"No, I haven't, but I've always wanted to come."

Kent looked oddly pleased. "I'm kind of glad that you haven't. I like being the one to take you for the first time."

Jane smiled at him. "I like that too."

Kathy, who had been clinging to Ed's arm, turned and looked at Jane as if seeing her for the very first time. She stood there, watching Jane smile up at Kent, and her eyes grew large.

"Jane," she said, "you've changed…"

But Kent was saying, "Would you like to dance?"

"Love to," Jane said. Then Kent's arm was around her, the music swept over them, and suddenly they were whirling across the floor, leaving Kathy and Ed behind. Jane looked back over Kent's shoulder and laughed at Kathy's amazed face.

"What are you laughing at?"

"Oh, nothing really. Just because I'm happy."

Kent said, "I'm happy too." He tightened his arm, and the music surged wild and sweet all about them. Other couples flew past like blurred figures in a dream.

I'm not dancing! Jane thought. I'm flying!

No dancing was ever like this! The music stopped and began again and stopped and began again. Some of the couples left the floor and others appeared.

A dark-haired boy touched Kent's shoulder.

"May I cut in?"

Kent said, "Well…"

Jane was dancing with the dark-haired boy.

"I'm Mike Ingram."

"I know. I've been in your chemistry class all year."

The boy shook his head. "You couldn't have been. I'd have noticed if you were."

"I sit three seats behind you. You should turn around once in a while, Mike."

"Gee, I really should!"

"Cut!" Another boy. "Hi. I know you, don't I? Girls look so different at dances; you know, all fixed up and shiny."

"I have the locker next to yours," Jane told him, "You've never even said hello in the mornings. I don't know whether I should dance with you or not." But the lilt in her voice made it clear that she was teasing.

"Well, you never said hello either, then," the boy retorted, "or I would have said hello back to you."

"You're forgiven," Jane said, "and I'm ashamed of myself."

Why, I never *did* speak to him, she thought. And I spent the whole year feeling hurt because he didn't speak to me!

"Cut!" It was Kent again. "Hey, you might save me a dance."

Jane laughed. "As many as you want."

The music stopped.

"Intermission, I guess. Would you like some punch?"

"I'd love some."

Kent seated her at a table and then stood looking at her for a moment. "You will be here when I come back, won't you?"

She laughed again. "Of course."

"I just want to be sure." He reached over and touched her hand. "Nothing like this ever happened to me on a blind date before. When Kathy told me about you, I never thought you'd be like this."

"Why?"

"Well, she said you were quiet and aloof, but a nice-enough kid. When a girl says that it usually means she can't think of anything better to say."

"May we join you?" It was Kathy and Ed.

Ed looked hard at Jane. "Golly," he said, "Kathy's right. You do seem different tonight."

Jane looked at Kathy and her heart sank, for Kathy's eyes were hard. On other blind dates Kathy had been sweet—almost too sweet—talking with Ed and the other boy and every now and then speaking gently to Jane, as though she were a child. But, on the other blind dates, Kathy had been the only pretty one. Jane had sat awkwardly apart, not knowing what to say and afraid to call attention to herself by saying anything at all. Never before had Jane's date looked at her the way Kent was looking at her now—never had Ed's eyes wandered from Kathy to focus on Jane. Before, Kathy had been a friend, but now suddenly she was a friend no longer.

"I have a cousin," she said coldly, "who has an overbite like yours, Jane. The dentist thinks she should have braces, but she hates the thought of it. You've had braces for so many years—do they feel as awkward as they look?"

Jane started to answer, but no words came.

"The poor little thing has freckles, too," Kathy continued. "It does seem a shame, doesn't it? Some people have all the hard luck when it comes to looks."

On any other night words as cruel as those would have shriveled Jane into a self-conscious heap, wordlessly fighting back tears. Now she found herself smiling. What did it matter how she had looked in the past?

"Oh, most girls have to go through these things," she said as casually as possible. "We can't all be blessed with your good looks, Kathy."

Kathy's eyes widened. She opened her mouth and closed it again. For once in her life she could think of nothing to say.

Kent broke the silence. "I'm getting punch," he said. "Want to come, Ed?"

"Yes," Ed said, "Good idea." He got up to follow Kent and then turned back to Kathy. "If I'd been Jane," he said quietly, "I wouldn't have been that polite." He turned abruptly away.

Kathy's eyes were blazing. "What are you trying to do?" she demanded accusingly of Jane. "Break Ed and me up? This is the last blind date I'll get for you."

Looking at her, Jane felt a surge of pity. What an unhappy girl she is, she though in surprise. How unsure of herself she must be if she is afraid to ask anyone attractive to double with her! Why haven't I noticed before? Aloud she said, "Don't be silly, Kathy. You're Ed's girl, and he's always been crazy about you."

Kathy didn't answer. Instead she turned her face sulkily away, and they sat in silence until the boys returned to the table.

"Here it is," Kent said, setting down the glasses. "They call it punch, but I wouldn't advise you to drink any of it—it tastes even worse than it looks."

Jane glanced at the foamy, purple mixture and mimicked the look on his face.

"I think maybe I can survive without it then. How do you feel about it, Kathy?"

Kathy didn't answer. Instead she turned pointedly to Ed and asked, "Shall we dance?"

Ed looked at her for a long moment—at the pretty, selfish face, at the pouting mouth, and then slowly he shook his head. "This time," he said, "I'd like to dance with Jane. That is, if you and Kent don't mind."

"Of course not," Kent agreed.

Ed took Jane's arm and steered her out onto the dance floor. They danced for a while in silence. Then Ed said, "Until tonight I always thought Kathy was swell—she's so cute and always seems to know the right thing to say. But seeing the way she's treating you tonight, I'm not so sure. I never knew there was this other side to her."

He sounded confused. Jane felt sorry for him.

"Kathy's the same as always," she told him. "Lots of girls forget themselves when the boy they're interested in seems to—to—" She stopped and blushed.

"Seems to be getting interested in somebody else?" Ed finished for her. "Maybe she's right. To tell you the truth,

Janie, I wasn't too keen on Kathy's getting you as a date for Kent. I didn't think you'd hit it off together. You've always seemed so quiet and serious and all tied up inside yourself. But tonight—I don't know what the difference is exactly. You just seem to kind of sparkle."

Jane was surprised. "Sparkle? You mean I look different, don't you?"

Ed shook his head. "No, you look the same—very nice—but that's not what I meant. It's something else."

"What?"

Ed shook his head. "Whatever it is, I like it. And so does Kent. Here he comes to cut in."

A moment later Jane was looking up into Kent's teasing face. "Hi, there, freckles!"

Jane smiled at him. She thought, Even if the wish hadn't come true—even if I still did have freckles—I wouldn't mind being teased about them by Kent. He makes freckles sound almost like an accomplishment.

"And all that talk about braces!" Kent was still grinning down at her. "Boy, I used to hate those things, but I'm sure glad now that I wore them."

"You wore braces!" Jane asked in astonishment. Somehow she had never imagined the calamity of braces happening to anyone as attractive as Kent.

"Up until this past spring," Kent answered without embarrassment. "Then I graduated to a nighttime retainer."

The orchestra swung into the last dance. Kent tightened his arm and laid his cheek against Jane's hair. The lights dropped low, and for a moment they were lost in the softly swinging mass of dancers, swept along by the music.

Then it was over.

"Hey, here we are! Ready to go?" Ed had his hand on Kathy's arm, but his eyes were for Jane. The crowd swept them out the door, and they tumbled, laughing, into the car.

It was on the ride home that Kent kissed her—a gentle kiss, shy and awkward and half-afraid.

"Jane," he whispered afterward, "you're not mad, are you?"

"No," Jane whispered back, "I'm not mad."

She felt somehow that she should be—that girls were always angry and injured when they were kissed on a first date—but tonight it was part of the magic.

She leaned her head back against Kent's shoulder. From the car window she could see the night sky, still heavy with stars. She wondered idly which was her star, but they all looked exactly the same, swinging together high over the earth.

And then the ride was over and Kent was opening the car door for her, and she was saying, "Good night, Ed— Kathy—thank you for including me."

Kathy did not answer, but Ed said, "Good night, Janie; I'll be seeing you—soon."

They paused a moment at the front door.

"Good night, Kent," Jane said softly. "It's been the love-liest time I've ever had."

"It has been for me too." He hesitated. "How about tomorrow? There's bound to be something we can do, even if it's just a movie."

"I'd love to do something," Jane said. And to herself she thought, how easy it is! There's nothing terrifying or complicated about it; it's the simplest thing in the world.

She went into the house and up the stairs. She could

remember other evenings when she had come home from a blind date and crept up the stairs to throw herself miserably on her bed. But that was before, when she had not been beautiful.

She slipped into the room quietly so as not to waken Alice and undressed in the dark. When she lay down on her bed she could still feel the magic, leaping and laughing within her, and when she shut her eyes she could feel the warmth of it all through her.

"Jane!" It seemed only minutes later that her mother's voice called her name. "Jane!"

"Yes?" she responded drowsily.

"Jane, telephone!"

Jane opened her eyes. "Why, I just got home a few minutes ago!" Then she saw that the room was flooded with sunlight and Alice's bed was empty.

"Goodness," she said, "I must have slept and slept!" She stretched and yawned and went stumbling downstairs to the telephone. "Hello?"

"Hi," Kent's voice said on the other end of the line. "I hope you don't mind my calling so early. It's just that it looks like a great day for the beach, and if we went early we could spend the whole day. Would you like to, Jane?"

Jane smiled at the eagerness in his voice.

"That sounds great," she said. "I can be ready in a jiffy."

"Gee, swell. I'll be right over."

Jane hung up the receiver and was starting for the stairs when she overheard her name. She paused and heard her mother's voice in the kitchen.

"It was for Jane," she was saying. "A boy—maybe the one she went out with last night! Our ugly duckling is blossoming at last!"

"Well, it's no wonder," her father's voice replied. "When she walked out that door last night, smiling and chatting with that Browning boy, I hardly knew her. It could have been a different girl."

Jane laughed with delight. It was the star! She thought. Even Daddy noticed the change!

She started upstairs and came face to face with the hall mirror.

"Hi," Jane whispered happily to the face in the mirror. She started on, then did a double take and turned back. She stood staring for a very long time—at the freckles and the snub nose and the braces. Her heart sank.

"I was fooling myself," she said dully, "all along. I probably knew, deep down inside; that's why I didn't want to look in a mirror. Wishing on a star can't change your looks. I knew it—but I wanted so badly to be beautiful, I made myself believe it." For a moment her disappointment was more than she could bear.

And then, through her misery, she heard her mother's voice.

"I know what you mean, dear. But it's not a physical change; it's something deeper than that—a kind of inner glow. A girl can go along for years, and then one day something will happen to give her confidence in herself. Maybe a boy will look at her in a certain way, or smile at her, or kiss her. It happened to Alice—remember?"

To Alice? Jane thought of her lovely sister, and suddenly her mind slipped back to a time when Alice was not beautiful—when Alice had wished on stars too. Why it's true! she thought, and wondered briefly, what had changed Alice—a look, or a smile or a kiss. She knew instinctively that Alice would never tell. It is a very private moment when a girl discovers that she is beautiful.

She looked again at the face in the mirror and smiled. The face smiled back, not its old, tight-lipped grimace, designed to conceal the unconcealable braces, but an easy, happy smile. *And it was beautiful.*

Jane turned away.

"Mother," she called, starting toward the kitchen, "may I borrow your swimming cap?"

(written at the age of 21)

* * * * * * * * * * * * * *

What can I say about "The Wish"? There's so much about it that is dated. How many girls today wear nylon stockings and carry evening bags? How many boys "cut in" at dances and use words like "swell" and "gee"? Only one phone in the house, and it's downstairs, where everyone can listen in on whatever you're saying? Swimming caps at the beach? And an understood rule that a kiss on a first date is socially unacceptable?

Yet despite those details, the premise of this story has held strong over the years and is as true today as it ever was: A girl who feels secure in the fact that she is beautiful creates her own aura of beauty which transcends any physical imperfections she may have.

P.S. We Are Fine

Dear Mom,

Bobby just swallowed a nickel and Janie is trying to make him cough it up. Aunt Sarah gave it him to make him good.

I don't much like Aunt Sarah. She looks like a horse when she laughs.

Hurry up and find a place for us to live so we can come there. What is it like in Philadelphia? Are the houses big?

The nickel just came up.

Love,
Tony

Dear Tony,

Your Aunt Sarah is a kind and generous woman, taking you children to live with her while Daddy and I are looking for a home here. Besides she is Daddy's older sister and you must be very polite, darling.

At the moment Daddy and I are camping out in a one-room apartment. I don't know how long we will be able to stay here because the landlady thinks her son might be moving back in with her.

How is the school there? How are you and Janie and Bobby? Write and tell me about everything.

Love,
Mom

Darling Mother,

School here is wonderful! There is the cutest boy in my English class! His name's Torchy, and he is a darling. He's already invited me to go to the movies with him, but Aunt Sarah won't let me. You see, Tony was horrid and told her I was in love with Peter Lawford, and now she won't let me go anywhere for fear Peter Lawford will kidnap me.

I have to share a room with Aunt Sarah and, Mother, she *snores*! But that isn't the worst of it. This morning when I got up, sitting right there on the table next to her bed was a glass of water with Aunt Sarah's teeth in it.

Bobby is being an angel, but Tony is perfectly hateful.

Aunt Sarah says a girl of fourteen is too young to wear lipstick. I'm not too young, am I, Mother? Please write and tell her I'm not. Everybody else here wears lipstick.

Love to Daddy.

Devotedly,
Janie

Dear Mom,

Do I have to eat liver, I mean when it's breaded and tastes like an old shoe? Aunt Sarah says I have to or I'll be anemic.

Love,
Tony

Dear Children,

Janie, I don't believe Aunt Sarah knows who Peter Lawford is, so why don't you explain that to her and put her mind at rest? And I don't know what to think about this Torchy. What is he like? You know we don't object to your going to the movies with boys your age, but we would like to know a little about them first.

Tony, dear, you really should eat everything that is put before you. Please be good and make Daddy and me proud of you. Do you like the school there?

Bobby, do you realize that your birthday is coming soon? What do you want for a present? Are you well, darling? Janie wrote that you were angelic. If you don't feel good, be sure and tell her.

> Love to you all,
> Mother/Mom

Dere Mothr,

a fir engine. a gote. a ise crème. a Indian suit. a flaschlite. a building set. grene cars that run on weels. a rist wach like Tonys. money. candy. gum. a bik. a wagne. a teeth that cums out at night like ant Sarahs.

> Love,
> Bobby, age 6

P.S. ANY THING ELS.

Dear Mother,

Torchy is utterly gorgeous! He is tall with curly brown hair and a heart-stopping smile. I sit across from him in class and it's just super! I think he likes me too a little bit. He's on the football team, and all the girls are crazy about him. Except for me, that is. I just take him in my stride sort of.

Please, please, *please*, write Aunt Sarah and tell her that I can go out on dates and wear lipstick.

I told Tony about Aunt Sarah's teeth, and he came in to look after she went to sleep last night. They weren't in the water glass though, and we had to look all around before we found them in a bowl on the window sill.

> Your loving daughter,
> Janet (not Janie)

P.S. Don't you think *Janet* sounds more exotic than *Janie*? I told Torchy my name was Janet.

Dear Sarah,

I can't tell you how grateful Robert and I are that you were willing to care for the children while we try to find a place to settle. We have been house-hunting all day. The landlady who owns the place where we're now staying says we will have to move by the sixth, as her son is moving back in with her.

Sarah dear, don't you think Janie is old enough to wear lipstick and have dates on Friday and Saturday nights as long as she's home by eleven? Also, Tony is terribly allergic to liver, especially breaded.

Thank you again.

> Your devoted sister-in-law,
> Alice

Dear Mom,

School here is okay and I met some cool kids. One has red hair and no teeth in front. I fought him. I won. Why don't I have six toes on one foot like Geezer? Geezer is cool. He gets detention all the time.

Janie has been acting funny lately. She's all the time making Bobby and me call her Janet, and she's always hanging around with a drip called Torchy. I don't see why. He may have muscles but he's ugly and needs a haircut.

Bobby broke a vase yesterday and Aunt Sarah was awfully mad.

I don't have to eat liver any more.

> Love,
> Tony

Dear Janie,

Well, we are out of the room we were renting. Daddy and I spent last night in a motel. We just *have* to find a place soon! Staying in rented rooms is not a nice way to live.

I've heard from unknown sources that you and Torchy are getting on rather well. I knew your father for a long time before I even let him kiss me. Take it easy, honey, and remember you are just fourteen.

> Love,
> Mother

Dear Mom,

Can I have a dog? I found one on my way home from school, and Geezer and I fought over him. Geezer won, but his folks won't let him have it. I took it home. I named it

Skunky because it is black and white. We hid it under my bed. Aunt Sarah doesn't know. We call it IT because we don't know whether it is a boy or a girl. Janie says to call it him and hope for the best.

Love,
Tony

P.S. Torchy was over again last night. He and Janie went for a walk and didn't come back until late and you should have heard Aunt Sarah. I didn't know old ladies could yell that loud.

Oh, Tony, how could you!

For heaven's sake, get Skunky out of the house before Aunt Sarah finds him! Darling, if Aunt Sarah gets upset and refuses to let you stay with her, we'll be in a terrible fix. Daddy is starting his new job next week, and he and I have located a house that actually might work for us. It's small, but in a nice area right across from a park, with public schools within walking distance and a bus stop at the corner. The problem is that we're not sure we can afford it. Property values here are much higher than we ever imagined. At the moment we are boarding with some very nice people who are allowing us kitchen privileges so we don't have to spend money eating out.

Love,
Mom

P.S. GET RID OF SKUNKY FAST!

Dear Bobby,

This is a birthday letter to say how happy Daddy and

I are that a certain little boy was born just seven years ago, and we do so wish we could be there to spank and eat cake. Are you having a party?

Daddy is sending your birthday money and I am sending a present.

You are being good, aren't you, darling?

> All our love for our birthday boy,
> Mother

Dearest Mother,

Torchy means little or nothing to me, so you needn't worry. It's only that he is so sweet and the way he calls me *Jan-et* is too adorable. But he's just a friend after all, in a very friendly way, I mean.

Aunt Sarah had something that resembled a fit yesterday when she discovered Skunky. She punished Tony and gave Skunky to the garbage man.

Bobby is sick from his birthday because he spent all his birthday money on candy. Aunt Sarah bought him a cake at the bakery and it was actually quite good. That gave Tony an idea, so he told her he would be twelve tomorrow so she would get him one too. I thought that a clever idea for an eleven-year-old boy. Tony can sometimes surprise you.

Must rush now, phone ringing, maybe Torchy.

> Love and devotion,
> Janet

Dear Tony,

Why did you let her find Skunky?

Every time I think of the little house I wrote you about,

the more it seems to be just what we need for our family. But the owner says if we want it we must place a down-payment on it that is more than we have right now in savings. Maybe we can work on the owner until he weakens. It's worth a try anyway. We truly do want that house.

How is Torchy? Has he been over recently? Not that I really care, of course, I'm just interested.

> Love,
> Mother

Dere Mother,
    cum home. I miss you.

> Love,
> Bobby, age 7.

P.S. the truk was nise. the gum was horid. I lik Skunky. scool is worser and worser. so is Ant Sarah.

> more love,
> Bobby, Age 7.

Dear Mother,

Torchy and I have had a fight and I hate him worse than anybody in the whole wide world. He went out with that horrid stuck-up Lucy Myers, and I told him a thing or two. I'll never, *never* go out with him again ever. Oh, Mother, what will I do? What did you do with Daddy when you were fourteen? Isn't there anything I can do to get him back? I know I'm prettier than she is.

I'm so miserable.

Report cards came out. Tony got "A" in arithmetic. He got "C" in his other subjects and "F" in Citizenship. "F" is failing. Bobby was good in everything and so was I, except French, of course.

I guess I showed Torchy. The blots on this page are where I spilled a Coke.

Janie (not Janet)

Dear Mom,

Skunky is back. What should I do? He ran away from the garbage man and sits outside and howls for me.

Janie and Torchy busted up. After he left, Janie cried and cried, and she scared Bobby, and he cried too.

Aunt Sarah's teeth aren't in the bowl any longer, they are back in the glass.

Geezer and I had another fight. He won. I put some blood in a bottle.

Love,
Tony

Dear Children,

Our little house has still not been purchased by anyone else, so there is a tiny chance that some miracle will occur and we can get enough of a loan to cover it.

I have an idea about Skunky. Why not give him to Geezer's mother as a present?

All my love,
Mom

Dear Mom,

Aunt Sarah is mad again. Yesterday Bobby was thirsty and he pickup up her glass before he remembered about the teeth. They fell on the floor and chipped.

Skunky is sitting outside getting hungrier and hungrier. Janie isn't fun any more since her fight with Torchy. She is cross and nasty.

> Love,
> Tony

Dere Mother,

write to me sometime. don't writ to Tony.write to me. I am good. I am always good.

> Love,
> Bobby, Age 7.

Dear Bobby,

I am awfully glad that you are good, sweetie. I hope you will always be that way.

It looks like we may not qualify for a loan in the amount that we need to place a down payment on our house. Meanwhile, other people have been looking it over, people who can probably afford it. But things will be all right, honey. If we can't get this house, we'll find another one just as nice.

How is Skunky?

> Love and kisses,
> Mother, age 16

Dere Mothr,

skunky is getting fat. why did you say love motr age 16??? you are fordy too.

> Love,
> Bobby

Dear Sarah,

I can't tell you how much your keeping the children has meant to Robert and me at this hectic time in our lives. We couldn't have gotten on without you. We were hoping to be able to immediately buy a house and take the kids off your hands, but I'm afraid it's going to take longer than we anticipated to locate a property we can afford. You won't mind keeping them just a little bit longer, will you?

Thank you so much.

Robert sends his love.

> Affectionately,
> Alice

Dear Mother,

I feel awful. I haven't been able to eat ever since Torchy and I broke up.

Something seems wrong with Skunky. He is the queerest shape. It could be my imagination, of course, but, if it isn't, how long will it take to really know?

Tony has a black eye. He fought with Geezer again yesterday.

> Ever yours,
> Janie

Dear Mom,

Things here are very uncool. It was raining last night so I let Skunky in to sleep with Bobby and me. When Aunt Sarah found out, she got mad and whacked me on the bottom and she isn't even my mom. Then Bobby knocked over her teeth on an accident she smacked him too, but not as hard. Then she started crying. I don't think Aunt Sarah is a very reliable woman, do you?

> Love,
> Tony

Dear Sarah,

We thank you with all our hearts for the kind offer to lend us the down-payment for the house, but Robert and I wouldn't feel right accepting it, especially after all you've done for us already. Your keeping the children has been a godsend. If you could continue looking after them for just a little while thought, we are sure to find a place that's not so costly.

> Gratefully,
> Alice

Dear Sarah,

You are a darling to keep insisting on helping us pay for the house, but we just couldn't. If you'll only keep the kids ....

> Your devoted sister-in-law,
> Alice

Dear Children,

Guess what! Aunt Sarah has offered us enough money to buy the house, and she insists on making it a gift. I know this is partly your doing, since she's become so fond of all of you and wants you to have a lovely place to live.

Aunt Sarah suggests that we come to get you at once. Would you mind leaving for Philadelphia next week?

> Love,
> Mother

Dear Mom,

Heck no! That would be swell. Only I wish Skunky could come.

> Love,
> Tony

Dear Mother,

How thrilling! Aunt Sarah truly is a dear old thing despite her odd ways.

Something wonderful happened last night! When Torchy found out we were leaving he said he was sorry about our fight and he'll write to me every day whether I answer or not and he'll save up his allowances so he can come visit us next summer.

And then he kissed me. Oh Mother, I couldn't stop him! I guess maybe I didn't want to stop him very much either.

Do you suppose our new house is large enough to keep a pet? Tony really likes Skunky a lot.

> Love,
> Janet (Janie to the family)

Dere Mothr,

yes I shood lik to go. I am reddy. I will tak my truk.

Love,

Bobby, age a millin and ate

P.S. that is a jok. I am rilly not a millin and ate. I am rilly 7. I no another jok I lerned at scool but you wood not understand . you are to old. You are fordy too but you said you are 16 and that is not a nice thing to say wen it is not tru.

Love,
Bobby, age 7

Dear Aunt Sarah,

We love our new home. It is swell. The school is swell too.

Janie is in love with Peter Lawford again.

Skunky had puppies just as we pulled into the Philadelphia train station. If you see Geezer, ask him if he wants one. Mom made the baggage man help get the puppies out of Skunky and he was not happy. We took them home in Janie's hat, the one I sat on.

I hope you are not too lonesome now that we're gone.

Love,
Tony

P.S. Mom is sending you back your teeth. Bobby packed them by mistake. They are all right except that a few are missing, but they are in the back and don't show much.

There is a boy at my new school named Kenny. He has a wart on his nose. And he can stick pins in his feet and not even feel it.

I caught a mouse. Mom won't let me keep him so I

am sending him to you to keep for me until we come to visit you again. I made holes in this envelope so he can breathe.

> Love again,
> Tony

> *(written at the age of 13)*

★ ★ ★ ★ ★ ★ ★ ★ ★ ★ ★ ★ ★ ★

Although I started submitting stories to magazines at age ten, I didn't begin to sell them until I was thirteen. "P.S. We Are Fine" was one of my first stories to be accepted. The magazine was *Calling All Girls*, and they paid me $25.00. To understand how stunned I was by that payment, you need to realize that back then the only way teenage girls could earn spending money was by baby-sitting. And baby-sitters charged 35 cents an hour.

I can't remember where the idea for this story came from, but I do know where it led me, for the characters and plot took up residence in my subconscious. Twenty-five years later they re-emerged in the form of a book called *Hotel for Dogs*.

And it didn't stop there. Over thirty years after that, *Hotel for Dogs* became a big-screen movie.

A writer's life is filled with the unexpected.

The Corner

"It's not so awfully far."

Joan was painting her nails, sitting sideways on the porch swing, and Rocky was sprawled on the top step.

"We could be back by supper," he continued coaxingly, "if we took the bikes."

Joan looked up from the nail polish.

"The beach isn't any fun this late in the year," she said practically. "It's almost winter. What could we find to do on the beach after swimming weather's over? And, besides, Paul might phone."

Rocky said, "Paul!" with the ultimate disgust of a twelve-year-old brother. "We used to have fun till you met that darned old Paul. You got a date with him tonight?"

Joan said, "To the Homecoming Game and the dance afterward."

She let her voice fondle the words, liking the sound of them, covering up the thin little twist of fear at the bottom of her stomach. The Homecoming Game—and dance—Paul …

Everything will be all right she thought. Everything has to be all right!

"Remember last summer?" Rocky said bitterly. "You

said you weren't ever going to be like that. Now you've forgotten."

"No, I haven't forgotten. I just was wrong last summer, that's all. I didn't know about lots of things then. I was just a kid."

"You were fourteen!"

"Well, it's different now anyway. I don't know why, it just is."

She concentrated on her nails again, and her mind went back to last summer, seeing it long and lazy and golden, stretching behind her. It was the same kind of summer they'd spent every year since she could remember. She and Rocky would put on their swimming suits and ride their bicycles to the beach. They would start early in the morning with a pack lunch. Occasionally, she went with some of the girls from school, and Rocky with some of the boys who lived down the street, but usually they went together.

It was easy and comfortable to go with your brother; you never had to bother to make conversation or look attractive. Sometimes they rode the entire distance in a companionable silence, each deep in his or her own thoughts. The road was bumpy, with daisies growing wild and ragged along the edges of it; and the whole day lay ahead, a lovely free summer day.

One day in particular she remembered. It was almost exactly like any other day, or had been at the time. They had left their bicycles as usual behind a dune with the basket of lunch and had run for the water. They didn't enter it slowly or gracefully, they plunged into it all at once with a great splashing.

Joan gasped at the sudden shock of the cold water

about her. Then she took a deep breath and struck out. She was a good swimmer. She swam easily and strongly, her body relaxed, her strokes clean and even. Rocky could go faster, but tired more easily. He passed her, churning water like a little engine; and eventually she caught up with him again and splashed water in his face and went on farther, swimming on and on until all her strength was gone. Then she relaxed on her back in the water and let herself float in.

When she reached the beach, she sprawled out in the soft, hot sand and let the sun bake her.

Rocky came over and threw himself down beside her.

"Hot," she said.

"Uh-huh."

"You'll freckle."

"So will you."

"What makes some people freckle and other people not?"

"I don't know," Joan said. "The way their skin's made, I guess."

"Anyway, I don't blister. That would be a nasty mess, wouldn't it, with puss oozing out all over?"

She said, "Your crawl looks better."

"I get tired too easy."

"You just need practice."

She stretched and they lay in silence, too comfortable to make the effort that came with turning their heads to talk. The sun was almost directly above them, hot and fierce upon their backs. The sands shimmered with golden heat. The sky was the only other thing in the world, and it went on forever, thin and blue from the sea to the dunes, closing in the world and making it complete.

Suddenly there were voices.

Joan was half asleep. She felt Rocky move and lift his head.

"Hey, Joanie," he said, "it's the Brighton boy from school."

Joan said, "Who?"

"That blond guy, the one on the football team. A girl is with him."

Joan opened her eyes and blinked.

"Where?" she asked.

"Over by the far dune. They're holding hands."

That was the first time she ever really saw Paul Brighton. Oh, she had seen him at school and knew him to speak to, but she had never really looked at him. Now he stood, facing in her direction, stocky and tan in lime green swimming shorts, his hair a shocking splash of yellow against his sun-darkened skin.

He met her eyes and smiled and raised his hand in casual greeting before turning back to the girl at his side.

"He waved at you!" exclaimed Rocky.

Joan smiled. "The fatal charm. You have an irresistible sister."

"Who's the gal?"

"Nancy Trousdale. Nice."

"Pretty," Rocky observed.

"Uh-huh."

She relaxed again, burying her face in the sand, not particularly caring about Paul or Nancy or anyone else. The sun was a gigantic force, boring its way into her, becoming part of her. If she could just let herself lie still long enough and let her mind haze with sleep she would become part of the sun.

Rocky said, "They're walking off. He's got a car parked over near our bikes. He's still holding her hand. She looks like she likes it." He reached over and touched her shoulder. "Joanie?"

"Yes."

His voice was suddenly worried. "You won't ever be like that, will you? You won't get all silly and dopey about some guy and hold hands with him and stuff?"

Joan said, "No, of course not."

"But I'm not joking. I mean, honest, you won't, will you?"

Joan said, "I'm not joking, either." She sat up. "Come on, Rocky," she said suddenly, "let's take a dip before lunch."

The water was warmer the second time than it had been at first. Joan washed the sand off and came out again. She stood on the beach, watching Rocky's head as it bobbed about, a black dot against the silver of the water. There was a slight wind, blowing along the beach and stirring the sand into little puffs that rose and fell back in waves. The wind was cold when it hit her wet suit.

She stood there, feeling the heat of the sun on her head and the cold of the wind against her body, knowing the delicious tiredness in her arms and legs, secure in the strength of her slim body. She felt apart from everyone and everything in the world, a being that had no place in a world of ordinary people like her mother and father and Nancy and Paul and the teachers at school. Even a little apart from Rocky.

"I am Joan!" she whispered to the wind and to the beach and to the sun. "I am Joan! I am Joan!"

She began to run, and in a moment Rocky had caught

up with her and was running beside her, and it turned into a race for the dunes and the picnic basket.

That seemed so long ago.

Joan inspected the drying fingernails and leaned back in the porch swing. There was still the touch of fear at the bottom of her stomach, the funny, empty feeling that wouldn't go away. But it would have to go away. The Homecoming Game—the dance—Paul!

Half her mind listened for the telephone, and the other half drifted back, taking thoughts at random and dwelling upon them so she would not have time to let the fear feeling get hold of her.

The summer was long and lovely, like every other summer. It was like a straight smooth road, coming from one direction; and the autumn was like another road, entirely different, coming from somewhere else. Somewhere the two roads joined and made a corner. Somewhere there had been a place to stand from which she could choose either direction she wished. But the corner had been passed without her even knowing that it was there; and, try as she would, she couldn't quite recall where the corner had been or when she had turned it.

School began, with the clamor of voices and the crash of lockers and the smell of books. The first full days were crowded with learning a locker combination, meeting new teachers and starting new classes.

It wasn't until the second week that she met Paul.

He passed her in the hall, walking along with his arms loaded with books. He smiled and nodded and was lost in the crowd.

Joan watched the back of his head disappear among

the dozens of other heads that bobbed back and forth between classrooms, and thought suddenly that he was very handsome, perhaps the handsomest boy is school. The next moment she wondered where Nancy was and why she wasn't with him.

For some strange reason she kept thinking of him again and again. During history class, while she was studying her chemistry notes, while the Latin translation lay staring from the page before her, she kept seeing Paul. Paul without Nancy.

Three days later she saw him again. She not only saw him, she found him walking beside her and carrying her books as she left school. She didn't quite know how it happened, only that she was glad that it had.

"Your freckles are fading," he told her observantly.

"Second-year Latin is enough to fade anything," she answered. "But they'll be back next summer, don't worry."

"I know," he said. "I saw you acquiring them, remember?"

She blushed. "I remember. I'm surprised that you do."

"Why wouldn't I? It's not every day you see a pretty girl lying on the beach beside her little brother."

"At least," Joan said pointedly, "it was my little brother," and she could have bitten her tongue off a moment after she said it.

"Oh," Paul said. "You mean Nancy?" and he frowned. "That's over and done with. Just a summer romance. You know how it is."

"Yes," Joan said. "Of course, I know." She didn't know in the least, but she felt happy that it was over and that Paul did not seem particularly sorry. She passed some of her friends and waved at them. She was very conscious of Paul walking beside her. She watched the girls' faces with a thrill of pleasure.

That was only the first time. He walked home with her the next day and the day after that, and by the end of the week it had become a regular thing. He took her to the movies on Friday night, and roller skating on Saturday. It was something she had never known before—having a good-looking boy's face a few inches above her own, and warm, boyish laughter after all her jokes, and a ready car to take her places, and a ready arm to open a door or carry books or guide her safely across the street. She was in a daze about how it had originated. Two weeks ago she never would have thought of such a thing and then, suddenly, it was almost as though it had been there always.

"That's the way things like this happen, I guess," she said to Rocky. "They just happen for no reason. But—but—oh, Rocky, Paul's so wonderful!"

Rocky said, "I don't like him. I think he's a dope."

But Joan could not make herself care very much what he thought, because the next week there was a dance. The first football game of the season—and the dance after it—and she went with Paul.

In thinking back, there was no clear-cut picture of the way the dance had been. It all fell into a rosy blur of music and dancers swaying to the rhythm and little tables with flowers and gay, colored streamers.

The ride home in Paul's car was a blur too, sweet and indefinably wonderful. There had been a moon. And he *had* kissed her. Even the kiss was hard to remember. It didn't stand out as a shining token, the way a first kiss is supposed to. He had kissed her a great deal afterward, and all the times got mixed up together. But she would always remember that he had kissed her, and she had worn flowers in her hair, and the seat had smelled of leather.

Perhaps, thought Joan, that was the corner. Yes, I do believe that was it.

The telephone rang.

Rocky jerked to a sitting position on the step.

"That's probably him," he remarked impatiently. "Why don't you go answer it?"

Joan clenched her hands in her lap until they hurt. I don't want it to be Paul, she thought wildly. Oh, please don't make it be Paul!

The phone rang again.

There was the sound of the receiver being lifted and then her mother's muffled voice. The voice rose in a greeting, responded again and fell into an easy conversation.

Joan felt an immense wave of relief.

"It's for Mother," she said.

"Look," Rocky said, "if you don't want to talk to him, why do you hang around? We could take the bikes and go to the beach and be back in time to eat. Of course we couldn't swim this late in the year, but that doesn't matter. We can ride down and fool around and come back like we always used to do. Maybe take our kites along and see if there's a breeze. Golly, Joanie, what's wrong with you? We used to always do things like that."

Joan said, "I don't want him to call, but if he does I want to be here. Can't you understand?"

Rocky said, "No. I think you're dopey as you can be."

He got up and sauntered around the side of the house.

"I guess I'll get my bike," he called back over his shoulder, "and go by myself. I guess I can go by myself as good as not."

From the living room there came the click of the receiver being hung up.

Joan thought, Maybe I shouldn't have done it. I know I shouldn't have. It's not the kind of thing a girl does, but I just couldn't see it fall apart and not do anything. I had to try! Oh, please don't let him phone and make some excuse and call it off! Give me this one more chance! Please!

There was no reason for its having cooled off, except that it had. There was nothing to point at and say, "What's wrong? What's the matter?" It had just slipped away quietly, in the same way it had sprung up. Joan couldn't understand it. In school, he was distant but polite. He simply wasn't around much. He smiled in a friendly way when he saw her, but he seldom found time to see her. He had football practice after school every afternoon so he didn't walk her home anymore, and she walked with a group of girls. For yers she had walked with girls and not minded at all; but now she was very conscious that they weren't Paul, and she minded very much.

There hadn't been any dates for a long time. Paul was always busy—always going somewhere, always doing something that did not include her.

The Homecoming Dance was the big dance of the season. It followed the biggest game.

Joan thought, He's bound to ask me! He *must* ask me!

But the days slipped by and he didn't. And then there was only one day left before the dance, and it was too late for him possibly to think of asking her.

That afternoon on her way out of school, Joan passed his locker. It was open, and Paul was standing in front of it, stuffing in a pair of gym shoes and a skivvy shirt.

Joan stopped.

"Paul?"

He raised his head and nodded.

"Hi."

"Walking home?"

"Nope. Football. You know that."

Joan said, "Sure." She took a deep breath. "Paul, is something wrong?"

He looked at her sharply. "No, of course not. Nothing's wrong. It's just that—oh, you know how it is."

"No," Joan said. "I don't know how it is. I—that is—the Homecoming Dance is tomorrow night, Paul."

She knew she shouldn't have said it. She should have let him call it the way he wanted it to be. But somehow she couldn't. Not like this. Not without even having made an effort to save it, when there was no reason for its being this way.

She said, "Are we going, Paul?"

He closed his locker.

He said, "I don't know, Joanie. I don't—"

"It's the big dance of the year! Or—" Suddenly the thought came to her. "Are you taking somebody else? Beth or Dolores or—or Nancy?"

"No," he said. "I'm not taking anybody else. It's not that. It's—well, okay. We'll go."

The world shone suddenly, wonderful and clear. She had won! One night was all she needed—one magic night like that first dance—and everything would be safe again. She knew it would.

"I'll be at the game, Paul, to watch you play. And I'll meet you at the door to the locker room afterward."

"All right," he said. "I guess that'll be okay."

It had been fine, perfect! Until that fear began to gnaw.

She thought, I know I shouldn't have made him say he would take me. But it was the only way! And I know I can bring it all back if I have tonight. Please let me have tonight! Please don't let him call it off!

Her fingernails were dry.

The phone rang.

There was a pause, and then her mother's voice called, "Joan!"

Joan took a deep breath and went into the house and picked up the receiver.

"Hello?"

"Hello. This is Paul."

His voice had the sound of a very young boy, carefully repeating a memorized speech.

"Hello, Paul."

Suddenly it didn't matter anymore. Whether they went or not didn't matter. Down deep inside she had known all along that there would not be another magic night. And now she didn't even care.

"Look, Joanie, I'm sorry, but I won't be able to take you to the dance tonight. My dad says I've got to get the car in early, right after the game. He wants it for something."

She thought, We could take the bus! But she didn't say it.

"I'll probably see you at the game," he went on. "I'll look for you in the stands. I'll probably see you there. Okay?"

"Yes," Joan said, "that's all right. That's all right, Paul."

She hung up the receiver and came back to the porch. Strangely there was no great bitterness or hurt. There was just numbness. She was over. The way Nancy had been over. A summer romance more or less—an autumn romance— what did they matter?

She thought of the summer, the long, golden summer stretching behind her, free of twisting little jealousies and tears, free of sudden sweet joy, free of agonizing moments of heartbreak that come so easily at fifteen and last such a short time and yet fill the world so completely while they last. Only she and Rocky, swimming and laughing and lying in the sand with the strong, hot sun beating down upon them the summer long.

She thought, I can go now and still catch up with Rocky before he reaches the dunes. I can take my bike and head him off by going through the short cut. It can be the same as it was last summer! It can be—

She was halfway down the steps before she stopped, knowing that it *couldn't* be the same. They could do the same things again, but she would no longer be "Joan." She would be "Joan, the girl Paul kissed." That would never be the same. And she and Rocky would not be the same, because between them would be the thin line that separates a child from a person who has passed childhood and is growing up. And all the while there would be an emptiness that would not go away.

Once you're around the corner, she thought, you can't go back. You can't ever go back again. No matter how much you want to, there isn't any way to go back. Only ahead.

Suddenly, she began to cry—silent, scared crying—a way she had never cried before. It wasn't for Paul. There would be other Pauls. But for something rather precious that had slipped away from her and been left behind—and lost forever—around the corner. On the other street.

(written at the age of 15)
Second Place Winner in *Seventeen Magazine's*
Creative Writing Contest, 1951

☆ ☆ ☆ ☆ ☆ ☆ ☆ ☆ ☆ ☆ ☆ ☆ ☆ ☆

At age fifteen, I fell violently and abruptly in love. His name was Vic, and he was eighteen years old and first mate on a fishing boat that my photographer parents chartered for a photo assignment off the Florida Keys.

From my diary: "Vic is a marvelous swimmer. He can stay under water over two minutes, though he cannot even breathe through his nose because he broke it in a fight. We docked in Key West, and oh, how painful it was to say farewell! I gave Vic my address, and he has promised to write me.

"He kissed me!"

So the Prince came at last and the dreamer was awakened. Just as in the tale of Snow White, the touch of his lips on hers did the trick. It wasn't a very long kiss, (after all, poor Vic couldn't breathe through his nose), but it was magic nevertheless. I waited in agony for the letters that did not come.

First love; first heartbreak. There was no returning to innocence. With the event of that kiss, I had turned the inevitable corner, and life would never be the same.

This story is not about Vic. It's about that turning point.

Bruce McCown's Sister

Bruce got home on a Saturday evening when we were at dinner. We heard the front door open and close, there were footsteps in the hallway, and all of a sudden he was there before us, big and broad-shouldered and handsome.

"Bruce!" Mother let out a gasp. "Good heavens, darling, what are you doing here? We didn't expect you home until Wednesday."

"What happened?" Dad asked, his face lighting up with pleasure. "Did they shove that final exam over so you could take off early?"

"I'm afraid not," Bruce said. "I've left school. I'm home for good." He set his suitcase down with a thump and began to take off his coat.

The room was filled with silence. We simply could not believe it. We stared at him, and finally I gave a shrill little laugh and said, "He's joking."

"Of course, he is." Dad's eyes were questioning. "You are, son, aren't you? You had us worried for a moment there."

"I wish I was," Bruce said. "Joking, I mean. I wish I could have thought of some easier way to break it to you. I've been trying, all the way down on the train, but—there isn't any other way. I've left school. I'm not going back.

There's nothing I can say to make it sound better."

"But, why?" Mother's voice came out in a whisper. "I thought you liked it there. We were all so proud when you got accepted at the Military Institute! How can you possibly just leave it?"

"It was either that or be expelled," Bruce said. "They gave us a choice. I wasn't the only one. About a third of the class left with me."

"Expelled!" Dad exclaimed. "Expelled for what?"

"For cheating." He had his coat off now and picked up his suitcase. "I'm going upstairs now. I'd like to get to bed. Can we talk about it in the morning?" His eyes were pleading.

"Don't you want some dinner, dear?" Mother asked gently. "It's your favorite—fried chicken."

"Thank you, but I've already eaten. I mean, I tried to eat—on the train. I'm not—very hungry." Bruce's voice broke and he turned quickly and crossed the living room to the stairs. We could hear his footsteps when he reached the hall above and the sound of his bedroom door closing.

In the dining room below the three of us sat and stared at each other. Then I jumped up and quickly began clearing the table. I knew that no one was going to eat anything more.

To understand the extent of our shock you must understand about Bruce—what he was to us and always had been. To me there had never been anything in the world as wonderful as being Bruce McCown's sister. I don't know about other brothers and how they treat their sisters, but to me Bruce had always been a confidant, a friend, and an adviser as well as a brother. From babyhood on, he was successful at everything. He moved through school like a skyrocket, blazing a trail, scattering stars behind him for me to step on as I followed along two years in his wake.

Lessons were easy because Bruce helped me. "Don't let that math get you down, Margy. I'll go over the equations with you."

Teachers were genial to me, for Bruce had been an "A" student and president of the Honor Society and the Student Council. "You're Bruce McCown's sister? I'm so glad to have you in my class!"

Friends were plentiful, for Bruce had paved the way for friendships. He had been voted "Most Popular" in his senior class, and the silver trophy for "Best All Around Athlete" stood in the case in the hall with his name engraved on it.

Glorying in his triumphs, I moved behind him, reaping the harvest of all his achievements. I was a success even before I started. Because of that, I couldn't believe, any more than Mother and Dad could, this terrible thing that had happened.

"It's a mistake," I thought. "It has to be."

But the next morning the headline ran the width of the Sunday paper: NINETY-THREE CADETS AT LAWTON MILITARY INSTITUTE FOUND GUILTY OF CHEATING.

"Ninety-three young men, members of the freshman class at Lawton Military Institute, were found guilty Friday of purchasing answers to this year's final examinations," the story related. "The answers, which were copied from previous years' examinations, were sold to the younger cadets by a well-organized 'answer ring' of upper classmen. Students guilty of purchasing those answer sheets were granted the privilege of withdrawing from the Institute. Members of the ring were expelled."

The final paragraph of the story was the clincher. "One of the freshmen to leave the Institute was a resident of Brownville, Michigan, and a former honor student at Brownville High School."

"Bruce is the only Brownville student attending the institute, and everybody knows that!" Dad exploded. "The paper ran a big article about him when he was accepted there. How can they do this without even calling him to see if the story has validity? I'll sue them! It's libel!"

"No, it's not, Dad," Bruce said flatly. "It would be libel if it wasn't true, but in this case it's just reporting the news."

"But it can't be true!" Dad exclaimed. "You couldn't have done a thing like that!"

"I did," Bruce said. His face was set and pale, but he met Dad's eyes directly. "I bought the answers, Dad, at ten dollars a sheet. There were four sheets—that's forty dollars it cost me. I took it out of my savings account."

"But, why?" Dad's face crumbled, and for one dreadful moment I thought he was going to cry. "Why, son? Why would you do such a thing? I don't understand."

"I did it because I wanted a high grade on that test," Bruce said. "I wanted it enough to cheat for it. I can't make excuses, because there aren't any. I was caught, and I deserved to be caught. I'm sorry. I'd give anything in the world if I could tell you it was a terrible mistake. But it wasn't. The truth is that I cheated, just like the most common sort of criminal, and if the paper wants to print a story about it they have a perfect right to do that."

After that there was very little left to say.

Everybody in Brownville knew about it by Monday morning. I could tell that at school by the strained silences and awkward greetings. Normally when trouble strikes a family, friends try to help them with sympathy and commiseration. In this case, however, that was all but impossible.

"Do you have the history assignment finished?" Ginny asked inanely when I stopped to get my books out of the locker we share. Ginny is my best friend and has been ever since grammar school.

"No," I said. "I didn't have time. Or, rather, I had time, but—" I decided to go ahead and bring the subject out into the open, "Our family's been kind of upset this past weekend."

"I can imagine," Ginny said awkwardly. "I didn't know how to say it but—well, you know I'm sorry."

"I know," I said shortly. "So am I."

The attitudes of my teachers varied from one class to the next. All of them had known Bruce and most of them had taught him. When I told Miss Martin, my history teacher, that I had not completed the assignment, she answered with the sympathy she would have shown if I had told her I was suffering from some terrible illness: "That's all right, Margy. Try to bring it in tomorrow." With Mrs. Burrows, who taught geometry, I felt as though I were the one who had been found guilty: "Keep your eyes on your own paper, Margy McCown," she snapped the moment I glanced toward Ginny to see if she had an extra pencil.

"I was only—" I began, but she stopped me with an icy stare.

"In this class," she said, "we work out our own answers. If we had kept a sharper eye on your brother when he was in high school, we might have instilled a sense of values in him which would have saved him from the scandal he's involved with today."

I felt my face flushing hot with anger.

"My brother—" I paused. What could I say in his defense or, for that matter, in my own? For all I knew, she might be right. Perhaps Bruce *had* been permitted to get away with dishonesty all during high school simply because of his open, likeable face and charismatic personality. Perhaps his actions at the Military Institute were only a continuation of habits established in earlier years which until now had gone undetected.

Miserably, I lowered my gaze to my paper and began mechanically checking over my answers.

At the end of third period the summons came for which I had subconsciously been waiting. Mrs. Burrows said, "Margie, Mr. Erickson wants to see you in his office."

I had been expecting it, but nevertheless a feeling of shock went through me as the words were finally spoken. I walked to the office slowly, feeling my knees strangely weak beneath me. Once inside, I was ushered immediately into Mr. Erickson's private cubicle.

Our principal is a quiet, gray-haired man who combines warmth with a sense of authority. I have never known anyone who did not like him. Bruce used to refer to him as "a really good guy."

Now, behind his flat-topped desk, Mr. Erickson regarded me solemnly.

"Sit down, Margy," he said. "I want to talk to you. I

read about your brother's—trouble—in the paper yesterday. I want you to know how deeply I regret what has happened. I know your parents must be terribly upset."

"Yes." My mouth was dry. "They are. We all are."

"I know that things must be especially difficult for you right now." Mr. Erickson's eyes were kind. "Something like this is bound to have its side effects. Bruce was a well-known personality at Brownville High School and this disgrace is bound to be gossiped about. There is little I can do to make this easy for you.

"I do want you to remember though that talk dies down almost as quickly as it arises. A scandal of this nature is a source of excitement for a little while, but before long something else comes along to take its place. Right now the sensation caused by that newspaper article has brought the situation to the forefront of everyone's mind. But after a little time passes the story will be old news, Bruce will go off to school someplace, and life will settle to normal again."

"Yes, sir." I was grateful for the words of comfort. "I guess you're right, sir."

"In the meantime, you just keep up your own fine work here. You are a good student, Margy. Of course, Bruce was too—an all 'A' student, as I remember—a fine boy, I always thought—" Suddenly his voice changed and the professional attitude seemed to drop away. He was simply a man, a friend, who had guided my brother and me through the greatest years of our development. The disappointment in his face was unconceivable. "What happened to Bruce, Margy? He had so much potential! Whatever made him do it?"

"I don't know," I said.

"There has to be a reason. A boy like Bruce—"

"I don't know," I repeated. "He just did it, that's all."

"I'm so sorry," Mr. Erickson said quietly.

The cafeteria was crowded, as always, and my stop at the principal's office had delayed me. Everyone else was seated by the time I arrived at the junior table with my lunch tray. By the silence that fell at my approach, I knew immediately what they had been talking about.

Then, suddenly, the conversation began again, a little too loud, about sports, classes, play rehearsals, the spring formal.

Ginny shoved her tray over to make a place for me. "Come on and sit down, Margy. That spaghetti looks good today, doesn't it?"

"Yes," I said. I looked at the spaghetti, and I knew I would not be able to swallow it. I looked at my classmates, and I could not bring myself to speak to them. Shame and misery rushed through me.

I cannot face it, I thought. I simply cannot face it.

"Excuse me," I said shakily. "I—I forgot something. I have to go."

Leaving my well-loaded tray on the table, I bolted for the door. And then I was outside.

Without stopping to think about what I was doing, I broke into a run. Wildly, blindly, I ran, leaving them all behind me—along the path by the fence, across the corner of the football field where the shadow of the bleachers fell in a dark splash against the sunlit ground, on past the pines, past the parking lot, off the school grounds. Frantically, without thought or planning, I ran, feeling the wind against my face, the hot sting of tears in my eyes, until at last I stumbled to a halt, overcome with exhaustion. There was, after all, no place to go, nowhere to escape from the thing that had happened. It was there all around me.

I could return to school or I could go home. I chose to go home.

"It will not stay this terrible," I told myself hopefully as I trudged down the sidewalk. "Just as Mr. Erickson says, people will forget about it." I recalled the words he had spoken there in the office. "After a little time passes the story will be old news, Bruce will go off to school someplace, and life will settle to normal."

It will, I cried silently. It will have to! Clutching that thought to me, I turned up the walk to our house.

There was no one in the living room when I entered. The house was silent with a strange, mid-day kind of emptiness. Dad was at work, I knew, and Mother, perhaps, was out shopping. I crossed the living room and went up the stairs, feeling like a stranger in this unaccustomed quiet, and started down the hall to my room.

Bruce's room was across from mine, and his door stood open. I passed it quickly, but not quickly enough.

"Margy, is that you? What are you doing home?"

I paused at my own door, my hand on the knob. For the first time in my life I did not react to Bruce's summons. I felt a rise of fury at his nerve in calling to me, this brother whom I had idolized and who was now responsible for so much misery.

"Don't worry," I said bitterly, "I haven't quit school, and I haven't been expelled. I'll be going back tomorrow. I have a—a—headache."

The words were hurtful, but I meant them to be that

way. It was with a fierce sort of pleasure that I saw the pain on his face as he appeared in his doorway.

"Margy," he said, "come in here a minute, will you? I want you to give our parents a message for me when they get home."

"A message?" I was startled despite myself. "What kind of a message, and why can't you tell them yourself?"

I hesitated a moment and then crossed the hall to his room. To my astonishment I saw an open suitcase on his bed, neatly packed with his belongings.

Bruce followed my eyes and nodded.

"I'm going away."

"What!" I exclaimed. "What do you mean, away? Where are you going? When?"

"Right now. As soon as I'm through packing." His face was quiet and set in determination. "Where—I don't know exactly. Anywhere. Maybe I'll enlist in the Army. Tell the folks I'll write them as soon as I get settled someplace. Tell them not to worry, that I'll be fine."

"But you haven't finished school yet!" I said in bewilderment. "Just because you've left the Military Institute doesn't mean you can't finish college somewhere. Dad will feel terrible. He's always expected so much of you!"

"With this on my record," Bruce said, "I could never get accepted at any of the big out-of-state colleges. And it would be too late to register anyway for this coming semester. The only thing I could do would be to get a job here in Brownville and register close by at the State University. I'd be right here on top of you. People would never forget me."

"How could you do it, Bruce?" I burst out suddenly. "Can't you try to explain it so I can understand? We've always been so proud of you! You've always been so wonderful!"

"That's just it," Bruce said. "You were always so proud of me—you and Mother and Dad, all my teachers at Brownville, Mr. Erickson, everybody. Bruce McCown, honor student—Bruce McCown, scholarship winner—Bruce McCown, President of the Honor Society! Well, in college Bruce McCown wasn't such a superman, Margy; he was one of a lot of supermen. He couldn't breeze along as he had in high school where everything was easy. In college he had to buckle down for the first time in his life and put everything he had into working. I couldn't do poorly there, Sis, not after all the glory in high school. Not with you and the folks all expecting so much of me."

"But you're smart," I said. "You could study. You could earn good grades anywhere, Bruce."

"I did study," Bruce said. "I studied like crazy. I got the subjects under my belt and I really felt I was mastering them. And then it was time for finals, and I learned about the 'answer ring'. That's when I panicked, because the other guys were using it. They were buying the answers, and their scores were going to be perfect."

"But why did *you* buy them?" I asked him. "Just because *they* did?"

"Like I told you, I panicked. That's the only reason I can give you. At the Institute they graded on a curve—a certain number of 'A's, a certain number of 'B's, a corresponding number of low grades. The guys who were using the purchased answers would push my grade to the bottom, no matter how hard I studied. The only way I could compete with them, I thought, was to get the same answers and get the same grade they did."

His face was lowered so that I could not see his eyes.

"It was the mistake of my life, Margy. I knew it the moment I'd done it. I got back to my room with those answer sheets and laid them on the bed. And then I looked up and there on the bureau was that picture of our family, the one we had taken at the lake last summer, with all of you standing there, smiling at me. I looked at your faces, and I knew I couldn't do it. I had the answers, sure, but I couldn't use them."

"You couldn't use them!" My heart leapt. "You mean you *didn't* cheat on the exam?"

"No, I didn't use them, but I cheated by buying them. I stuck the sheets in my bureau, under my clothes, planning to get rid of them. But before I could, the school found out about the ring and got the names of all the freshman customers. Then they searched our rooms and, of course, they found the evidence."

"But you didn't use them!" I kept repeating the glorious statement. "Couldn't you tell them that? Couldn't you explain it to them?"

"That didn't matter, Margy. I bought them. Can't you see how that made me as guilty as anyone? I meant to use them. It was just the accident of glancing up at that picture at just the right moment that prevented it."

"Well, if you're guilty," I said, "you've been punished for it. And you didn't run away from your punishment. Why are you running now?"

"Because my being here is punishing you as well, Sis—you and our parents. You're suffering too, and that isn't fair."

"It's as fair as it was for us to glory in all your triumphs," I said.

The knowledge rose within me, a wisdom of which until now I had been incapable. An acceptance of my own faults and weaknesses as well as my brother's.

"We're a family," I said. "You made a mistake—we all make them. But we see each other through things. That's what a family is for, not just for the good times."

I reached for his hand, as I had done so often in my childhood, when something was wrong and he could fix it. My big, wonderful brother, who could do anything! Except that now I knew that he was not really perfect, he was merely human.

"Bruce," I begged, "please, don't leave! Please, stay with us! We'll get though this somehow, all of us together!"

There was a moment's silence. His face was doubtful.

"Are you sure?" he asked. "Is this the way you want it?"

"It is," I said. And I meant it.

It would not be easy; I knew it would not be easy. Not for Bruce, or our parents—not for any of us. It would be weeks, months, perhaps years before this "trouble" would be forgotten. But, eventually it would be. And in the meantime we would face it and, through facing it, we would grow stronger.

I drew a long, slow breath and looked at my brother, at the real and beloved person beneath the glorious exterior.

"I am proud," I said. "I will always be proud—of being Bruce McCown's sister."

(written at the age of 16)

Unlike most of the stories I wrote during my teens, "Bruce

McCown's Sister" bore no relationship to my own life. The plot was spurred by a newspaper article about a prestigious military institute from which two-thirds of the freshman class had been expelled because of cheating. My mind leapt from the young men themselves—"Whatever could have possessed them?"—to their disappointed and disillusioned parents. And from there to the boys' siblings. How would they react?

What happened to families who dealt with this sort of disgrace? How would I feel if one of the cheaters was my brother?

Stop Calling Me Baby

There are eleven maple trees between our house and the Tutters', eleven maple trees and thirty-two cracks in the sidewalk. The summer that I was fifteen the maple trees were green and full and their shade fell in large, dark patches across the hot sidewalk except in the morning when it fell in the street. I must have walked up and down that sidewalk a thousand times that summer, always slowly, always casually, looking at the maples and cracks in the cement.

"Where are you going?" Vandy asked as I pushed back my chair from the table and started to get up.

"Out," I said shortly.

"Where?"

"For a walk."

Mother said, "Karen, you've hardly touched your dinner. Is something the matter?"

"No," I said irritably. "Nothing's the matter. I just want to go out for a walk. Does anbody have any objections?"

Vandy said, "I'll come with you." She got up too. Vandy was eleven.

"No," I said furiously. "You will not. I'm going by myself."

Vandy's blue eyes filled with tears. She said, "You're

horrid. You're always horrid; you never let me do anything anymore."

Mother said, "Karen, don't you think—"

I left the room and went out onto the porch and slammed the screen door behind me. It was early evening. The sun still slanted through the trees and fell halfheartedly on the pavement, the way it does on summer evenings when the dark comes slowly and there is a muffled clatter of silverware and a blur of voices from open doors and windows.

The Tutter house, almost at the end of the block, was larger than ours, although Mr. and Mrs. Tutter lived there by themselves most of the time, with the girls now married and Joe away at college. I had never been inside, but I was sure I knew how it would be; a hall and then a living room with a piano which Mrs. Tutter sometimes played, and beyond that the dining room. Upstairs the master bedroom faced out over the lawn, and Joe's room was on the first floor around to the side.

Joe was in the driveway washing the family car.

I concentrated on the trees as I passed him—ten—eleven—twelve—and I went on slowly to the corner and around it. I stood there quietly for a moment. Then I turned and started back.

This time, as I passed, he said, "Hi."

I looked up.

"Hi," I said.

He was bent at a stiff, awkward angle, holding a rag in one hand and the hose in the other, washing the whitewalls. He was wearing an old pair of khaki pants, which covered his legs to the ankles, and a stained white T-shirt. I deliberately kept my eyes from his right leg and focused instead on his bristly crew cut and the nose that was bent a little sideways from football.

"Where are you going?" he asked in a friendly way.

"Nowhere special," I said. I crossed over and stood beside him, watching him. "When did you get home?" I asked, although I knew.

"About a week ago. I got a ride down from school with some of the fellows."

"Have a good year?" I asked.

"Sure." He looked up at me and grinned. "What's new around here? Let's see, you must be about in the ninth grade by now, right?"

"Tenth," I said, hating him.

"Tenth? Well, gee!" I hated him more than ever.

He straightened slowly and stood back to inspect the tire. He gave it a final slosh with the hose. Then he wrung out the rag and went to turn off the water.

"See you around," he said.

I watched him turn off the faucet and walk up the steps—moving stiffly with one hand on the railing—and go into the house. I heard his voice in the living room, saying something and then laughing, and then heard his mother's laughter. A few minutes later the light went on in his room. I watched the light for a long time and when it finally went off I turned and began to walk hurriedly away. I didn't want him to come outside again to find me still standing there.

It was dusk now. The sun was gone and there were no more shadows, but it was hot. Some little girls were playing hopscotch in the street in front of our house.

Vandy broke away from the group and came over to me.

"Do you want to play?" she asked. She wasn't mad anymore. Vandy never stayed mad.

"No," I said. "I don't."

"You haven't played all summer!"

I started to walk away, and then I turned back.

"Okay," I said. I tossed in my stone, hopped across the course, turned and hopped back. I picked up my stone and tossed it into the next block. "There," I said, "now I've played. Now leave me alone."

"Okay," Vandy said, "okay. Gosh, you don't have to be so snotty about it."

I went into the house and through the living room and upstairs to my room. Mother and Dad were sitting in the living room, but they didn't say anything as I passed through. I went into my room and closed the door and lay down on the bed. I hadn't eaten much dinner and I was hungry, but I was hungry in another sort of way too. It was a kind of aching feeling, a loneliness that wasn't really loneliness but something else, a feeling of being incomplete. It was a feeling that had started this summer, and it was mixed up in my mind with the heat and the twilight and the maple trees and the children's voices in the street outside.

But it wasn't those things, I thought. Those were a part of every summer I had ever known—they were nothing new. And Joe was nothing new either. He had lived up the block for as long as I could remember. He had washed the car dozens of times and cut the grass and flown airplane models in his front yard, and I had hardly noticed. Even that time two years ago when he had been in the automobile wreck—it had been after his senior prom, and I had heard my parents talking about it afterward: "The Tutter boy...what a shame...to lose a leg at eighteen...and I hear he was offered a football scholarship...such a nice, attractive boy...such a terrible pity..." I had been sorry, of course, but the pain had not been my pain. I was too busy playing hopscotch with Vandy in the street.

I got up and turned on the light and went over to the dressing-table mirror. I looked at myself for a log time. Then I took off my jeans and shirt. I went over to the closet and got the blue taffeta dress Mother had given me for Christmas and put it on. It was too heavy for summer and a little long; I had never even had it on long enough for Mother to turn it up on me. I went over to my bureau and searched through a top drawer until I found a lipstick.

Vandy came in.

"What are you doing?"

I said, "I thought you were playing hopscotch."

"I was." She came closer. "What are you getting dressed up for?"

"Just because I feel like it. Don't you ever knock before you come into somebody's room?"

Vandy ignored the question. She stood on one foot, as though she were still playing hopscotch.

"They're talking about you downstairs," she said. "Dad says you're acting like a brat this summer and ought to have your bottom whacked even if you are in high school." She smiled importantly. "Mother says to leave you alone. She says you're just going through a stage."

"I am not!" I said angrily.

"Mother says you are. She says all girls go through it

at one time or another. I won't though." She looked at me more closely. "Gee," she said, "you look funny in that dress. Your stomach sticks out."

I turned to her in fury. "Yours does too," I snapped, and added, "and *you've* got a broken front tooth."

Vandy's hand flew to her mouth.

"I don't," she wailed. "It's only a baby tooth." She was dreadfully self-conscious about her chipped tooth.

"It's not," I said cruelly. "It's a permanent tooth, and it's broken and can never be fixed, and someday it will die and turn black, and the dentist will have to pull it, and you'll have a big hole there."

"It won't!" Vandy screamed. "It won't!"

She started to cry and ran out of the room. I watched her go with a stab of guilt. No one in our family ever mentions Vandy's tooth.

I turned again to the mirror. The girl who looked back at me couldn't be called pretty, but she did look different— older—with the bright slash of lipstick across her mouth. I sucked in my stomach as tightly as I could, and the dress didn't look bad at all, really.

"Joe," I said softly, experimentally, "darling." The sound of my voice saying the words frightened me a little. It was so clear-cut and definite when it was put into words that way. I let myself picture his face, the funny, bristly hair and the clear blue eyes, and my throat tightened. "Joe," I whispered again, "I know how hurt you must be—how lonely— how empty life must seem for you after being a big football hero and everything. You can talk to me—I'll understand. I'll try to comfort you."

There was a rap on the door.

"Karen?" Mother's voice was brisk. "I want to talk to you."

I didn't answer, and she opened the door anyway and came in. She looked angry. Then she saw the dress and the lipstick, and for some reason her eyes softened.

"What do you want to talk about?" I asked her.

"You know very well," Mother said, sitting down on the end of the bed. "Vandy's in her room crying her heart out because you teased her about her tooth. You know how hard Daddy and I have worked to get her to stop worrying about it."

"Well, that's tough," I said. "Real tough for Vandy. You act as if she's lost a leg or something. If the only thing she ever has to worry about is her tooth, she'll have an easy life."

Mother stared at me as if she hadn't heard me correctly. Then she said, "Baby, what's the matter with you this summer? I don't think I've ever heard you say a thing like that before."

"Nothing's the matter with me," I said, "and, please, stop calling me 'baby.'"

Mother said, "Karen—" and suddenly, unreasonably, my eyes flooded with tears.

"Leave me alone," I said. "Why can't everybody just leave me alone?"

I pushed hurriedly past her and ran downstairs, through the living room and out onto the sidewalk again.

It was night now, but not really dark because of the lights from the houses and the street lights, and the eleven maple trees were huge dark masses against the night. I walked quickly, not bothering to count them. This time I knew I wasn't going to walk casually past the Tutter house.

There was an ache inside me almost too great to bear, and I knew I had to see Joe. It didn't matter if he thought I was completely crazy. I had to see him or I'd die.

I didn't stop to think about what I was doing. When I reached his house I walked quickly up the porch steps and knocked loudly on the door.

Mrs. Tutter answered it. She came from the living room, calling something laughingly back over her shoulder. She peered out uncertainly through the screen, not recognizing me on the dark porch.

"Yes?"

"I'm Karen Jackson," I said. "From down the street."

"Oh! Well come in, dear," Mrs. Tutter said pleasantly. "Is it Girl Scout cookie time already?"

I felt my face flush bright red.

"No," I said. "I just—just—" I had an inspiration. "Mother is baking and she's run out of eggs. She wanted me to ask you if she could borrow a couple."

"Why, yes, of course." Mrs. Tutter said graciously. "Come in, Karen, and I'll get them for you."

I followed her through the hall and into the living room. It was just the way I had imagined it, spacious and pleasant, with a huge piano in the corner. Mr. Tutter was watching television, and there, sprawled on the sofa, was Joe.

"It's the little Jackson girl," Mrs. Tutter said as though she were introducing me for the first time. "Her mother's baking and needs some eggs."

Joe looked up and smiled. "Hi," he said. "I'd hardly have recognized you out of jeans."

"Hi, Joe," I said.

Mr. Tutter nodded at me and turned down the volume of the television. "Some of these summer replacements are better than the regular programs," he said.

"Yes," I said, "I guess they are."

Joe hauled himself up and motioned for me to sit down at the end of the sofa. The cushion was warm where his good leg had been. He said, "What are you all dressed up for, Karen? Got a heavy date?"

"No," I said, and then added carefully, "Not tonight."

"Well, you look awfully nice anyway."

"Thank you." Happiness rushed through me. It was almost too much to believe that a moment ago I had been moping in my bedroom and now here I was, sitting in Joe's home, right on the sofa beside him.

I made myself look at him straight on. His eyes were as blue as ever, and his crooked nose made him look endearingly vulnerable. I longed to take the rough brown head and draw it down to my shoulder and say aloud the words I had practiced in my room.

Someday, I thought. Next summer, perhaps, or the summer after. He is looking at me now and smiling; it is a beginning.

Mrs. Tutter came bustling back into the room. She had a dish in her hand.

"Are two eggs enough dear? Are you sure that's all your mother wanted?"

"Yes," I said. "Two eggs."

Joe glanced toward the window.

"It's pretty dark out. Maybe I'd better walk you home."

I thought for an instant that my heart was going to stop beating.

"You don't have to do that. It must be hard for you—I mean to walk any more than you have to—"

"It'll do him good," Mr. Tutter commented gruffly, his eyes still plastered to the television screen. "He's so restless that he's about to tear the house down this summer. Wish Marcy had come home with him as we asked her to."

"She couldn't," Joe said. "You know that. Her mother wants to take her shopping in New York."

"Don't see why she can't get her trousseau here as well as in New York," Mr. Tutter muttered, but there was a note of teasing in his voice. "The way women carry on, you'd think the poor girl was getting something special instead of a gimpy, flat-nosed college student with two years to go for his B.A. She must be crazy!"

"She is," Joe said, "about me. Lucky girl didn't even have to run very fast to catch me. With this damned fake leg I couldn't get away from her."

He grinned and his father chuckled and shook his head. It was evidently a familiar exchange. I stared at them both in bewilderment.

"Marcy?" I said. "Who's Marcy?"

"Joe's fiancée," Mrs. Tutter explained. "No matter what those two jokers say, they don't mean a word of it. Pop's just as crazy about her as Joe is."

"Fiancée?" I repeated the word numbly. "You're getting married?"

"This fall." Joe swung his good leg off the sofa and got a grip on the arm. He held out one hand. "Want to give me a haul up, Karen?"

I shook my head. "No."

"No?" He looked surprised.

"You don't need to walk me home." My voice was ragged and strange to my ears, like somebody else's voice. "I like to walk by myself. I like to walk in the dark."

As instant later I was in the hall groping blindly for the door.

"Karen?" Mrs. Tutter's voice flowed after me. "Your eggs!"

The world seemed to be spinning around me. For a moment I clung to the doorknob; then with a tremendous effort I turned and went back into the living room and took the dish with the eggs.

I said, "Thank you."

At home I undressed quickly and got into bed. The sheets were cool. I didn't even bother to turn off the lights; I just lay there feeling the dull ache, the funny, throbbing emptiness. Outside a faint breeze stirred the maples and they rustled, a whispering of leaves moving a little in the summer night, and I thought, "There are eleven maple trees between our house and the Tutters'." Which was a silly thing to think because it didn't matter how far away Joe was, eleven maples or eleven million miles.

I was still lying there with the light on when Mother stopped by my room on her way to bed.

She hesitated in the doorway.

"Karen?" she asked. "Are you awake?"

"Yes," I said.

Mother said, "I thought you might have fallen asleep with the light on." She came over to kiss me goodnight the way she always did, just as if I were a baby or something. But this time was different. This time I did not mind.

"Mother," I said, "Joe Tutter's engaged. He's getting married."

"Oh, baby," Mother said softly. "I'm so sorry." From the way she said it, I knew she understood, that she had understood all along. Suddenly I was crying; deep choking sobs, the way I had not cried for years.

"I love him!" I cried. "I love him so much!"

"I know," Mother said. She did not put her arms around me; she merely sat there and let me cry. "It's so hard," she said, "the first time you love somebody. I remember. It's hard."

"It's not the loving that's hard!" I cried angrily. "It's the other part! It's wanting him to love me too!"

Mother was silent a moment. When she spoke again her voice was very gentle.

"That will come in time," she said. "They don't always come together, you know—loving and being loved. If they did, there would be no chance for us to grow."

I leaned back against the pillows. Outside the maples moved again, and the breeze slipping through the window was surprisingly cool, almost an autumn-flavored breeze. I drew a long, shaky breath.

"It has been a horrible summer."

"It has," Mother agreed. "For all of us. And the worst of it is, we still have it to live through with Vandy."

She smiled, and suddenly to my amazement I found myself smiling back. We sat there for a long time after that, not mother and child the way we had been, but two old friends who had found each other again after a long time apart.

(written at the age of 16)

✩ ✩ ✩ ✩ ✩ ✩ ✩ ✩ ✩ ✩ ✩ ✩ ✩ ✩

When I was fifteen, our family spent the summer in Atlanta, Georgia, where my parents were on a photo assignment for a travel magazine.

There were maple trees lining the sidewalks in the neighborhood where we rented a house for that summer, and in the evenings after dinner I would go for walks. People would be sitting on porches or washing cars in driveways or mowing lawns, and there was always a crowd of children playing hopscotch in the street. On my way home it would be darker, and the people would be fewer. Lights would go on one by one in the houses. The mothers of the children would call them in, one at a time, until the street was empty.

In the house across from us there lived an attractive young man who had lost a leg in an auto accident. He was usually outdoors in the early evening, working on his car or doing yard work. One time when I walked by, there was a girl with him and they were laughing together.

Of such raw material are stories made.

I was not in love with the one-legged boy in Atlanta. I never even met him. But I knew, or thought I knew, what it would be like to be in love with him. I empathized with the girl who was laughing with him in the driveway, and years later the heroines of two of my young adult novels would fall in love with physically handicapped boys. In *Ransom* it would be a young man whose arm was wasted by polio, and in *Stranger with My Face* it would be a boy who had been badly burned.

The original title of this story was "End of Summer." My main purpose for writing it had been to recapture the sensations of that Atlanta summer—the slowly deepening twilight, the rustle of the maples, the children's voices ringing out through the dusk. I had never before lived in a well-populated neighborhood. Our beach house in Florida was set back from the road, surrounded by sand dunes and sea boats. The idea of so many people living so close together with their lives spilling out through their front doors into the warmth of the summer night was enchanting to me.

My editor changed the title to "Stop Calling Me Baby." When I complained, she said firmly, "A title must hook the reader's interest. 'Stop Calling Me Baby' suggests intriguing conflict. 'End of Summer' sounds like a pile of dead leaves."

I still liked "End of Summer" better. But I'd learned by then that a writer seldom wins when she argues with her editor.

The Reason

Up until a few moments ago his mother had been there, but now she had slipped from the room, very quietly, thinking he was asleep. The boy was glad she was gone. A woman was warm and comforting, but he did not want to be comforted. A woman's hands were gentle and her crooning could partially smooth away the pain, but he was no longer a child and he wanted to bear his pain. He was suddenly a man, and he had no need for mothering.

The boy lay stiffly on the bed and felt the cold cut easily through the coarse blanket and wrap itself about his body. He thought about the calf and shut his eyes and imagined himself in the barn, sprawled beside it in the warm, sweet-smelling hay. He could almost feel the heaving of its hot, awkward body and smell the strangely beautiful smell that he always connected with it. Of course, all calves smelled a little the same, and they were all built in much the same way, but somehow this one had been different. This one was *his*.

It was the first time he had even been allowed to witness a birth. Always before he had been too little, but because his father had promised that it was to be his calf and because he was now quite old, all of twelve, his father had said it was all right. His mother had tried to dissuade them. She hadn't wanted him to see what giving birth was like. She herself had gone inside the inn and stayed there while the actual miracle was taking place.

The cow had stood there, gasping a little—and then it had happened. There had been one crucial, heart-stopping moment, a moment in which the stable had seemed to vibrate with pain. And then, little and wet and helpless, there had been the calf. The boy had crept close and stretched out his hand and touched it very gently, and it had been real and alive beneath his touch. It was then that he had known that it was his calf, *really his.*

Now he turned and pressed his face deeper into the pillow. He was a man. He had loved something and it was gone. Such things happened all the time to men. They did not cry. They did not act like children.

At first he had been able to carry the calf, but to his disgust it had grown faster than he had. Somehow they had been alike. They had both had knobby knees and both had liked to drink from streams and run in clover. And they both had been born.

Lying there, he tried to imagine himself being born. He tried to imagine his quiet, comforting mother experiencing that brief moment of exulting pain that he had witnessed in the barn, but he couldn't. Still it must have happened or he wouldn't be here.

And someday he must die, as the calf had died.

"Why?" he agonized. "Why? Oh, why?"

Even his father had not known why. There had seemed no reason for it. None of the other cattle had been sick, only his calf. For two nights and three days they had worked with it, struggling against the icy wind to the stable where it had lain, feeding it by hand, sitting with it by night.

And today it had died.

They had carried it out to the edge of the woods, his father and he, and left it there. The wind had been stinging upon their backs as they stumbled along with the weight of the calf's body. The boy had wanted to dig a grave, but the ground had been too hard, and he had wanted to stay for a while beside it, there in the protective shelter of the trees, but his father had not allowed that. Instead they had returned to the inn. They had fed the other livestock. They had eaten dinner and seen to the guests. There had been no reason why the calf should have died. No reason at all.

The boy was glad that his mother was gone now. She was like all women. She stroked his forehead and dried his tears and told him there had to be a reason, that there was a reason for everything, that maybe when he was grown and thought back on this, he would see a reason and be able to understand something she herself could not explain.

It was his mother who had given it away about the empty stall in the stable when the people had come to the door. His father never would have thought of it. In fact, he had already told them there was no room, that the inn was filled. The people had turned to leave when his mother came forward and touched his father's arm.

"Wait!" she had said urgently. "You can't do this! You can't send them out on a night like this one. Especially a woman who is—who is—"

His father had shaken his heard, regretfully but firmly.

"There is no room," he had said.

The night was very cold. The wind, blowing in through

the open front door of the inn, was a sharp, icy wind.

"What about the stable?" his mother had suggested. "The calf died today. There is an empty stall. It would be better than bearing a child outside without shelter, out in the night, in the cold."

There was a moment of silence and the boy had tried to speak, but the words would not leave his throat. He wanted to do something to stop it. He wanted to scream at her bitterly, "The calf is dead! Isn't it lucky my calf is dead! What would we do if the calf were not dead!" He wanted to laugh wildly and convulsively, but he could not.

His mother's face was gentle, and the woman turned to her with quiet, trusting eyes. A look passed between them.

His mother had said, "You are very blessed."

The woman had said, "I know."

The boy had broken away and fled to his room. He lay very still upon his bed, trying to weep, but the tears would not come. There was only pain. He felt his thin body stiffen with fury against his mother. She had acted almost as though it were a fortunate thing that the calf had died. *His calf!*

The night was still. The only sound was that of the wind singing around the corners of the inn. After a while the wind seemed to die down and even this sound stopped. Everything was silent, a breathless sort of silence. The entire world seemed to be waiting for something.

The boy felt the waiting, the tension. He felt it in the air and in the pressure of the blanket upon his body and in the pulsing of his blood as it pounded through his veins. He heard it in the night and in the cold and in the stillness. In the terrible stillness he could hear the night singing a strange bewildering song which echoed louder and louder in his ears. He heard his breath, and his breath was singing, and he felt a pressure like the weight of the world.

Suddenly his hate and pain vanished in a tremendous realization! The moment was an exact duplicate, only a thousand—no, a *million*—times over, of that moment out in the hay when the cow had given birth. It was a moment of terrible glorious exulting pain, something he could not understand and did not wish to understand, but could only feel.

The door to his room opened and his mother came in. She crossed to his bed and spoke to him.

"Are you awake?" she whispered.

He heard her perfectly, but he did not answer for fear he might break the glorious spell that hung upon him.

She turned and went to the window and stood there a long time, looking out. Finally she came back and put her hand on his arm.

"Are you awake?" she asked again.

The boy sat up and got out of bed. The floor boards were cold beneath his feet, but he hardly felt him.

His mother said, "Hurry to the window and see."

He obediently crossed to the window. The singing was all about him and within him, throbbing in his ears, and the sky above the stable was burning as bright as day, lit by a star so brilliant that it might have been the sun.

"It's almost," he whispered to his mother, "as if the whole world were beginning!"

And then, quite suddenly, he knew the reason.

(written at the age of 14)

☆ ☆ ☆ ☆ ☆ ☆ ☆ ☆ ☆ ☆ ☆ ☆ ☆ ☆

When I was twelve, my dog was run over.

She was an Irish terrier named "Ginger", and I received her on my seventh birthday. At the time she was killed my parents were out of town, and my brother and I were under the care of our grandmother. When I got up that morning I called Ginger so I could feed her, but she didn't come. When I went out to catch the school bus, I found her body in the road.

The agony of that day was intensified by the fact that my mother wasn't there to comfort me. My grandmother tried, but it was not the same. I overheard her on the phone, canceling out of her regular afternoon card game.

"Lois is so upset," she told her friend apologetically. "You know how devastating life's little tragedies can be at her age."

I was furious. A little tragedy! Was that what it seemed to her?

"If this is a 'little' tragedy," I remember crying, "then how do people ever live through big ones?"

"With difficulty,'" my grandmother said.

In retrospect, I can see how that question must have affected her, as she had recently lost both her husband and youngest daughter. At the time, however, all I could think about was how heartless she was. Ginger was dead, and my grandmother considered it unimportant.

When my parents returned two days later, my mother wept with me.

"Why?" I kept asking. "Why did it have to happen? She was such a good dog!"

"There must be a reason," Mother told me. "You can't see it now, and I can't either, but it must exist. Maybe someday, when you look back, you will find that something good did come of this."

"That's impossible!" I cried.

But I grew up a bit on that day.

It was quite a while before I again felt like writing, and when I did I wrote "The Reason."

One year later, when the pain of my loss had receded, I submitted that story to a magazine called *Senior Prom*. They not only bought it, but made it the lead story in their December issue. An editorial comment beneath the title said: "This story is the work of a girl of fourteen. We are proud to open our Christmas issue with it."

The Silver Bracelet

Marilyn sat perched on the edge of her bed, waiting for the doorbell to ring. She knew she looked nice—not gorgeous, but very nice—in the soft, blue dress and black shoes and the silver clasp on her soft light hair. And, on her wrist, the bracelet.

The bracelet was heavy and cool against her skin. She studied it as she waited—the thick silver chain, the heart-shaped clasp, the smooth, shiny top that said "David". She knew that if she turned it over it would say "Marilyn" on the other side, but it was silly to turn it over because she would only turn it back again. The "David" was the important part.

"David," she said experimentally.

The name sounded familiar because she had said it so often in the past, yet now she could hardly remember the sound of his voice or the way he looked when he smiled.

But she could remember his face when he gave her the bracelet.

The night had been crisp and cool and filled with the smell of cedar smoke and the rustle of footsteps, muffled in tired, dead leaves. David had come to say good-bye. He was leaving for college the next morning, and he brought her birthday present because she would be sixteen the next day. They had walked along the dark sidewalk, scuffling their feet in the soft piles of leaves, holding hands and not saying much because there was nothing left to say. Down the street somebody laughed, and the laughter came, sharp and clear through the night, with the smell of fresh gingerbread and the blur of a phonograph.

David said, "It's been fun this summer."

Marilyn said, "Yes," and held his hand tighter, wishing she could call back the summer and hold that fast as well, even into the very heart of autumn.

The summer had brought the miracle, the startling realization, "David likes me!" and with that the unbelievable knowledge that no matter how many parties there were she would never need to sit home again because David would ask her, "Busy tomorrow night?" and all she would have to do would be to say "No" and he would take her. There had been laughter and moonlight swimming and the amazed glances of girls who had never bothered to notice her before and suddenly discovered that she had been chosen by David Bruster.

The summer had been the miracle. Now David was leaving for college on the morning train and taking the miracle with him. He wouldn't be home again until Christmas vacation.

"By the way," David said suddenly, "happy early birthday. I brought you something."

Then it was in her hands—the narrow white box with the top off and the tissue paper pushed aside—and the bracelet shining before her.

"Here," David was saying eagerly, "let me put it on for you," and his hands were fumbling with the clasp, and then it was on her wrist, lovely and unfamiliar and filled with magic.

"David," Marilyn whispered, "Oh, Dave, thank you!"

In the morning he was gone, but his going hadn't hurt so terribly. He had left a piece of himself behind for her.

The next day Marilyn wore the bracelet to school. The girls gathered around like chickens being fed, gasping and nudging each other and asking questions.

"David gave it to you? Why, Marilyn, I had no idea he was so serious about you!"

"We went steady all summer," Marilyn replied placidly.

"Yes, I know. But I can't picture *David* giving somebody a bracelet! He's always seemed so shy!"

"He isn't when you get to know him."

"No, I suppose not. Well, congratulations."

"Yes," the other girls echoed, "congratulations!"

Marilyn smiled and said, "Thank you," and touched the bracelet lightly with the tip of one finger, spelling out the D-A-V-I-D. David. Such a nice name. David and Marilyn.

A few days later, in leafing through one of the "character books" that were the latest fad, she came across her name listed with David's on the "cutest couple" page. Perhaps it was because she did look almost cute these days, her eyes dancing and her smile breaking forth at odd moments like a burst of sunshine. Or perhaps it was only because there were very few couples established and going together that early in the school year. But in the months that followed, all the "cutest couple" pages listed "Marilyn and Dave," even when people began to forget what David looked like.

Neither of them was much on letter writing. Marilyn's letters always began, "How are you? I am fine," and David spent the first half of each letter apologizing for not having written sooner and the second half promising to do better next time. But he would say, "I miss you," or "I dreamed about you last night" and sign it, "All my love, Dave." That made up for a lot.

When the Homecoming Dance came and Marilyn did not have a date, she wasn't lonely and miserable as she had been in previous years.

"Going to the dance tonight, Marilyn?"

"Nope. Looks like I sit home and write Dave."

"Of course. I forgot for a minute. Don't you wish he was here?"

"Yes, but he'll be home for Christmas vacation. I can wait."

"You certainly are being faithful."

"Well," Marilyn said lightly, "David's worth waiting for."

She looked at the bracelet, smooth and shining on her wrist, and she didn't mind missing the Homecoming Dance at all.

Christmas vacation finally did arrive with the sparkle of tinsel and the smell of fir trees. And David came home.

He was home three days before Marilyn knew about it, and even then it was by chance that she saw him at all. She was standing on the corner waiting for the bus, her arms piled high with packages. A tall blond boy crossed the street toward her and hesitated, and when she looked up she found his gaze locked on her face. Then she realized who it was.

He hesitated a moment longer and then came over to her.

"Hi."

"Hi, Dave."

They stood there awkwardly for a few moments, trying to think of what to say next.

"When did you get home?"

"A couple of days ago. I was going to call you, but I've been pretty busy."

"That's okay, so have I. How was school?"

"Okay. I'm glad to be out though."

"I guess everybody is."

"I guess so."

The bus arrived. They both saw it at the same time and waited silently as it approached. Then they smiled at each other, funny, embarrassed smiles, and David said, "Well, I'll see you around," and Marilyn said, "Sure," and got on the bus.

She found an empty seat and leaned back as the bus started. She could see David through the window; he had turned away and was walking rapidly in the opposite direction. There was no singing in her, no excitement, no disappointment, just an odd detachment and the thought, why, he's not nearly as handsome as I remembered him!

The next day David came down with the flu and spent the remainder of the vacation in bed.

The girls were very sympathetic.

"Oh, Marilyn, what tough luck! And after waiting so long, too! I bet you feel awful."

Marilyn smiled bravely and fondled the bracelet. When she was alone she still touched the bracelet gently, caressingly, and then she took it off and placed it in the top drawer of her dresser.

"I don't care about Dave anymore," she told herself calmly, "and he obviously doesn't care about me. He wouldn't have taken me to the holiday parties even if he hadn't gotten sick."

She felt empty and lost; not because she didn't have David, but because abruptly she didn't have anybody. She left the bracelet lying in the drawer.

It remained there until New Year's.

The New Year's Eve party was the most thrilling event of the season. It was held by the Tri-Hi-Y; there were hats and balloons and a big name band from out of town, and everybody who was anybody attended it.

Barbara was planning to wear the new rose-color formal she'd gotten for Christmas.

Bev was going with Ned.

Christia's mother was going to lend her the family pearls, real ones with a diamond clasp.

The girls spent hours on the phone or at one another's house hashing over ever detail.

"How late will your folks let you stay out?"

"Maybe till two if I push very hard. Is Ernie getting his dad's car?"

"He'd better, that's all I can say. You know, somebody said Alice Pitzer was going to be asked!"

"Oh, how funny! Who would ask her?"

"It's a joke, of course. Nobody would ask out a loser like big fat Alice, but everyone who isn't downright *odd* is going."

Marilyn, who stood near the center of the group, flinched.

"I'm not going," she said.

"Oh, that's different." The girls dismissed it fondly. "Everybody knows about Dave's being sick. You're not staying home because you're such a geek that nobody will take you."

One of the other girls laughed and slipped an arm around Marilyn's waist. "You've got his bracelet," she said teasingly. "You needn't worry about people thinking you're not wanted."

Eyes went automatically to Marilyn's wrist and then rose to regard her with astonishment.

Marilyn blushed and dropped her eyes with a flush of guilt.

"It's at home," she said in confusion. "The clasp broke and I haven't had a chance to get it fixed."

The moment passed and the tension vanished.

Talk went back to the party again; gay, cruel, happy talk, and Marilyn was still part of it, safe and secure in its midst. Less popular girls wandered past alone or formed aloof, envious groups of their own, but Marilyn was accepted and safe within the inner circle.

The next day she wore the bracelet again. It shone on her arm—a small, silver badge of honor that said to the world, "I am here to prove that this is a girl that somebody wants! This is a girl who belongs!"

Vacation ended, and school began again with its usual clamor. The weather was clear and cold, and there were skating parties and winter picnics and sleigh rides. Sometimes Marilyn went to the parties and talked and watched couples enjoying themselves, but she never had a date herself. The boys didn't seem to notice her.

And then, one day, one of them did.

She was sitting on a bench at the edge of the pond, buckling her skates. The boy was not a particularly handsome one—he had freckles and a snub nose—but he skated like a dream and he had the kind of smile that made you smile back whether you knew him or not.

Marilyn didn't know him, but she smiled anyway.

"Hi," he said without further introduction. "Are you any good at figure skating?"

"No," Marilyn said truthfully. "Not a bit good, but I can try."

The boy laughed and held out his hand.

"That's all it takes," he said, "a little trying and a patient partner. Come on, I'll go easy on you."

They skated slowly and carefully around the edge of the pond. The boy's arm was sure and strong and he knew what he was doing. After the first few minutes, Marilyn relaxed completely and let him lead her, fitting her strokes to his long, even ones.

"There," he said. "You feel better now, don't you? I'm not going to try anything fancy or let go suddenly."

Marilyn said, "I know. I'm just out of practice."

"You don't come to the pond often?"

"Not too often. I'm always afraid of falling down and breaking my neck."

The boy seemed to find that amusing.

"You don't need to worry," he said. "You won't break your neck when I'm around."

By the time they reached shore someone had a fire well started and some weary skaters were gathered around it, roasting hot dogs on sticks. The boy forced his way through the group with a display of valor and emerged several minutes later, mussed and sooty, but victorious.

He handed Marilyn a hot dog with pride.

"You know," he said awkwardly, "I've seen you around, but I don't even know your name."

Marilyn accepted the frail-looking hot dog with gratitude.

"It's Marilyn."

"Mine's Jack. Hello, Marilyn!"

"Hi, Jack!"

The party was a great success. They toasted marshmallows and drank cocoa from thermos bottles and then they roasted chestnuts in the embers. They told ghost stories and sang silly songs, and when the moon rose they walked home in a flood of silver through the snow.

The evening was perfect for Marilyn until the final moment.

That's when it happened.

"I had a great time tonight," she said softly to Jack.

"So did I," he said enthusiastically. "It's been swell. Would you like to go again next weekend, as my date this time?"

Before she had a chance to reply, Marilyn heard an answer given for her.

"Hey, Jack, you're poaching! Marilyn's private property!"

She turned quickly. It was one of the girls from school, her face surprised and indignant, as though an important rule had been ignored and she was seeing to it that things were placed in order.

The rest of the crowd heard her and with one accord they were surrounding them—laughing, teasing, heartless.

"Marilyn's spoken for, Jackie boy. Better luck next time!"

"She's Dave Bruster's steady girlfriend. Everybody knows that."

"Oh, Marilyn, I'll tell Dave when he gets home!"

For one crazy instant, on seeing the bewildered look in Jack's eyes, Marilyn wanted to turn to them all and shout, "No! No, I'm not Dave's girlfriend! That was over long ago. I just didn't want all of you to think I'm another Alice Pitzer—somebody no one wants—always on the outside of every group, all alone!"

She almost shouted it. But she didn't. Instead, she simply stood there silently, letting them chatter.

"See! She's wearing his bracelet!"

The band of silver had slipped down from beneath the sleeve of her jacket and sparkled bright in the moonlight.

Jack looked at it and then up at Marilyn.

"Oh," he said. "I didn't realize."

Then he smiled, a carefully careless smile, as though it hadn't really mattered at all.

"Too bad," he said. "That 'Dave' is a darned lucky guy."

That was all. There was nothing to say, nothing to do. She saw him at the pond several times after that, alone at first and then with an assortment of different girls. The hurt really came when it was one special girl, over and over again. Marilyn watched them sometimes as they circled the pond together. The girl was an even worse skater than Marilyn, but she was cute and unattached and she laughed a lot, and her admiring brown eyes said that there was no other boy in the world but Jack and that he was wonderful.

In the days that followed, Marilyn found a kind of loneliness she had never known before.

"I might at least have had a chance," she told herself miserably on one of these endless Saturday nights when she sprawled on her bed, trying to read. "It came so close, and we could have had so much fun if I could only have had a chance. It isn't fair."

Her voice cracked, and to her horrified ears it sounded like the voice of a very old lady.

"I'll grow old," she wailed, "and wrinkled and awful with gray hair and skin flapping under my arms the way old ladies do, and I'll still have to ride along on an old, used-up romance, and it's not *fair!*"

She buried her face in the pillow and cried. It was the first time she had cried since that time that seemed so long ago when she had taken in the full reality of the fact that David was going to leave her and go off to college.

"It's not fair!" she sobbed over and over.

The phone rang.

Marilyn lay still, waiting for someone else to answer it.

It rang three more times, and then it stopped.

A few minute later there was a rap on her door.

"Marilyn," her father said, "it's for you."

Marilyn sat up quickly and dabbed at her eyes with a corner of the bedspread. Her heart jumped in a crazy rhythm against the walls of her chest.

"It's Jack!" she thought wildly. "It's Jack! I know it's Jack! Maybe he's tired of that girl and has decided he doesn't care about David, and he's calling me anyway!"

She opened the bedroom door and raced down the hall to the telephone stand at the head of the stairs. The phone was off the hook, lying on the table. She stood looking at it a moment before she picked it up.

"Hello?" Her voice cracked again and she chided herself silently for having been crying.

"Hello, Marilyn? This is Sally."

The breath went out of Marilyn with a little sigh. With a violent effort she kept the disappointment out of her voice.

"Hi, Sally."

"Hi! Look, Marilyn; I don't know how you're going to feel about this, but I thought I'd ask you anyway."

"Yes?"

What did it matter what she asked? It wasn't Jack.

"Well, my cousin Jimmy is in town. He came down from college for the weekend and doesn't know anybody here. I have a date with Tom tonight, and I wondered if you'd like to come along as a date for Jimmy." She hesitated and then rushed on. "I know how it is with you and David, and if you don't want to go just say so and I'll understand. But my folks won't let me go out and leave poor Jimmy just sitting there, and everybody else is booked up, and I thought with Dave away and all you might want to come along, just once, for something to do."

Marilyn smiled grimly, picturing the long lonely evening that lay ahead of her, just like every other Saturday night for the past year.

"Sure," she said. "I'd be glad to come. What time will you be by for me?"

"Is about half an hour from now all right?"

"Fine. Thanks for thinking of me."

She replaced the receiver and went to her room to get changed. She felt no excitement. This was a date of convenience, "just once, for something to do," nothing more than that. And it wasn't with Jack.

She dressed quickly without thinking much about it.

The soft blue wool dress. The black shoes. The silver clasp in her hair. And, of course, the bracelet.

Then she sat on the edge of her bed, waiting for the doorbell to ring.

Before long there was the sound of a car in the street outside her window. The engine grew quiet, and a car door opened and slammed shut.

They're here, thought Marilyn. Sally and Tom and Sally's cousin—they're here.

It wasn't until that moment that the realization struck her, hitting her with such a jolt that it tore away the carefully constructed wall of disinterest as though it had never existed.

David was forever away—one bright summer millions of years ago. Jack was a mere glimpse of something that might have been and still might someday be. But the stranger she was about to meet was *here right now* and real and very important. Charming or dull, good-looking or homely, he wasn't just a dream or a memory; he was a flesh and blood boy, probably pleasant since Sally was pleasant and he was her cousin, and could be danced with and talked to and used to create memories of his own.

Here is my chance, she thought with wonder. My chance to break away! Here is the chance I've been waiting for!

She took off the bracelet. For a moment she felt a rise of terror—a miserable, helpless, all-alone sort of feeling— as though her protective shield had been yanked away from her.

Then she caught sight of herself again in the mirror. She looked nice—not gorgeous, but very nice. Quite nice enough to be of interest to any normal boy.

She smiled at the girl in the mirror and that girl smiled back at her. Then she took off the bracelet and placed it in her top drawer along with her freshman class picture and outgrown training bra and the medal she had won in a poster drawing contest. It was a fine bracelet, but it had served its purpose, and now it was time to go on to other things.

"Goodbye, David," she said and closed the drawer.

Then she went downstairs to answer the doorbell.

(written at the age of 17)
Third Place Winner in *Seventeen Magazine's*
Creative Writing Contest, 1952

☆ ☆ ☆ ☆ ☆ ☆ ☆ ☆ ☆ ☆ ☆ ☆ ☆ ☆

I wasn't a "Marilyn", thank God. I did at one time wear a boy's ID bracelet, but we soon broke up and I handed it back with no regrets.

However, I knew plenty of "Marilyn"s who hid their social insecurities behind their silver bracelets, class rings, letter sweaters and other tokens of affection from boys they were dating.

The interesting thing about this story—other than the fact that those same insecurities affect teenage girls today—are the little things that depict a particular era in teenage society. How many young people today even know the term "character books"? Not many, I bet. In my teenage years, those notebooks were secretly passed from student to student, under cover of our desks, so we could rate each other in regard to popularity. "Prettiest Girl"," "Homeliest

Girl", "Handsomest Guy", "Smartest", "Dumbest", "Sloppiest Kisser", etc. I was part of all that nasty activity and considered it fun. Today, I am filled with guilt about our unthinking cruelty. I cringe when I imagine how many unpopular young people read the unkind things that were written about them and went home to consider suicide.

I wish things were better today, but I'm afraid they're not. Technology has replaced "character books" with Face-Book and Twitter, and the slurs that are posted there can be read, not only by classmates, but by anyone and everyone.

And rather than bragging about their romantic relationships by wearing I.D. bracelets, girls are getting tattooed with their current boyfriends' names. In this story, Marilyn was able to dispose of the bracelet once she faced the fact that she was ready to move on. But a name etched into one's body is there forever.

Detestable Dale

"Ronnie Chandler asked me to the Fourth of July dance," I said contentedly.

It was a good time for confidences. Mother and Dad were out playing golf and my brother Dale was over at the bowling alley. Susan and I had the house completely to ourselves, and we were sitting in the living room playing records.

"Swell," Susan responded dutifully. She picked up a record and concentrated on the label. Then she turned it over and carefully read the other side.

"Well, you might sound a little more enthusiastic," I said in a hurt voice. After all, Susan is my best friend, and even if we both knew in advance that Ronnie was going to ask me, she might have shown a little interest when it finally happened.

"I'm sorry," she said quickly, laying down the record. "I'm really awfully glad for you—honestly I am."

Her voice was funny and low and not at all like Susan's.

"What's the matter?" I asked in surprise. "Fred Stevens invited you, didn't he?"

Fred Stevens was the captain of our school football team, and everybody in town knew he was going around in circles about Susan. She's the kind of girl who's head cheerleader and the sweetheart of every club in school. If she weren't my very best friend, it might not be too hard for me to become just a little jealous of Susan sometimes.

"Oh, yes," she answered dully. "Fred did ask me a couple of days ago. I told him no."

"You what?!" I gasped in amazement. Girls just don't refuse dates with boys like Fred. "What did he say?"

Susan smiled in spite of herself.

"It was really kind of funny," she said. "He was so surprised. He said I'm the first girl who ever turned down a date with him, and if I he couldn't go with me, he wasn't going to go with anybody. I guess I should have said yes. It's just—" she hesitated and then burst out—"oh, Lyn, sometimes a dance just isn't worth going to if you aren't going with the right boy."

"You don't mean you're in love!"

I was astonished. After all, as Susan's best friend I certainly should have known.

"What difference does it make? He doesn't care anything about me."

"Then you *are* in love!" I exclaimed triumphantly. "Who is he? Tell me. Do I know him?"

She picked up a phonograph record and began to turn it idly around and around in her hands. "You know him."

"How well?"

"Awfully well."

"Who?" I stopped suddenly, not able to believe it was possible. "You don't mean Dale?"

Susan nodded, concentrating very hard on the record. Her face was red.

"But, Dale! My goodness, there's nothing romantic about Dale!"

"Well, of course, you wouldn't think so," she said. "He's your brother."

I frowned and thought about Dale, trying to visualize him from Susan's viewpoint. He is tall, of course, but terribly thin—Mother is always telling him to finish his dinner—and he has long eyelashes which he hates. But aside from that he is just detestable. He has enormous clumsy feet and always leaves his clothes strewn all over the floor and never polishes his shoes. When he was little he used to collect frogs and eat raw potatoes. And the way he's always talking about sports, you'd think he was a mighty athlete or something, but really he wasn't even able to make the second-string football team; he had to settle for bowling instead. There is nothing—absolutely nothing—about Dale to make a girl like Susan fall for him.

"I've liked him for ages," she was saying, still not looking me right in the eyes, "ever since we were little and he used to tease me, remember? But now that we're older he never even talks to me any more. He acts as if he doesn't know I'm alive."

"It's not just you," I said comfortingly. "He thinks dating is silly."

Susan raised her head and looked at me, and I was amazed to see that there were tears in her eyes.

"Lyn," she said miserably, "if Dale doesn't ask me to the Fourth of July dance, I don't want to go. Isn't there anything you can do?"

"I don't know," I answered doubtfully. "I don't have much influence with Dale. But I'll try."

After Susan had gone I sat there in the living room, thinking about the situation, and it kept seeming sillier and sillier. Here was Susan, who could go to the dance with a boy like Fred Stevens, wanting to go with Dale! There is nothing even faintly romantic about Dale. He is my brother, and I should know. I guess a girl knows her own brother.

But I had made a promise and I intended to keep it. At dinner that night I brought up the subject of the dance.

"I'm going with Ronnie Chandler," I said.

"Darling!" Mother is always wonderfully thrilled at the right times, and she knows what a dream Ronnie is. "How marvelous! What are you going to wear?"

"I don't know," I said, glancing sideways at Dale. "What do you think I should wear, Dale?" It was the only way I could think of to get him into the conversation.

"What?" said Dale. All three of them stared at me in astonishment.

"For heaven's sake, Lyn," Dad said finally, "why ask Dale? You know he's not interested in things like that."

"Well," I said, "I just thought it was about time he got interested in that sort of thing. After all, he's a year older than I am, and a boy who's a senior in high school ought to have more social consciousness."

Dale turned to me in horror.

"Gee whiz!" he said. "What's got into *you*? I guess I can handle my own 'social consciousness' without any help from you."

Dad immediately nodded agreement. He and Dale always stick together. But Mother frowned thoughtfully.

"I don't know but what Lyn's right," she said. "Why

don't you ask someone to the dance, dear? You would probably have a wonderful time."

"You could always ask one of my friends," I added quickly. "What about Susan, for instance? She's one of the most popular girls in the junior class."

Dale's face got purple with rage. He pushed back his chair and got up from the table.

"I'm not going to the dance," he roared. "I don't like dances. You've got your own date; what are you worrying about me for?"

He turned and stalked out of the room.

"Dale!" Mother called after him. "Come back and finish your dinner, dear! You're getting so thin—no wonder you didn't make the team!"

But Dale was already out in the hall and we could hear him stamping up the stairs.

The next morning at school I reported my lack of progress to Susan. She did not look happy.

"You know what the trouble is?" I said. "Dale probably doesn't think of you as a girl at all. To him you're just his kid sister's friend. No boy is going to feel romantic about somebody like that."

"I think I could make him think about me as a girl," Susan said softly, "if I could just go out with him once."

Looking at her, I couldn't help but agree. No boy, even Dale, could go out with Susan and remain immune to her. Suddenly I had an inspiration.

"Fred Stevens *did* say he wasn't going to the dance with anyone else, right?"

Susan nodded, puzzled. "He said if he couldn't take me he wouldn't go with anybody. Why?"

"Because," I said happily, "I have a marvelous plan. Listen, we'll tell my family that Fred asked you—everyone knows he was going to anyway—and I'll say we're going to double date and you're spending the night with me. Then, at the last minute, Fred can get sick. There you'll be, all dressed for the dance with no one to take you. Dale will have to do it!"

Susan looked doubtful. "What if he doesn't?"

"He'll have to," I assured her. "Mother will make him."

She shook her head, still doubtful. "I don't like it. I want Dale to ask me because he wants to."

"I know," I said impatiently. "But you know as well as I do that once the two of you are out together and the ice is broken, he'll have a great time, and next time he'll ask you himself."

"Well," Susan said without much enthusiasm, "maybe you're right."

I could tell by the tone of her voice that she was not completely convinced and it was more than likely she would change her mind at any moment, so I immediately began to put the plan into effect. At dinner that night I again brought up the subject of the dance.

"Susan's spending the night here," I said casually. "We're doubling."

Dale glanced at me suspiciously but when I did not even glance in his direction he relaxed and concentrated on his mashed potatoes. The die was cast.

The rest of the plan worked beautifully, just as I had known it would. Susan arrived on schedule. We went to my room, locked the door, and settled down to plan our attack.

"Does he suspect anything?" Susan asked nervously.

"No," I assured her. "Of course not. What could he suspect? It's not like you don't spend the night over here all the time."

"I don't know," Susan said. "It's just that—oh, Lyn, if he ever found out I'd just die!"

"He won't find out," I insisted. "Don't start losing your nerve now—there's no time. You have to start getting dressed."

Susan gave me a last desperate look, opened her overnight bag, and began to take out her underwear and cosmetics. Her dress was spread on the bed. I smiled encouragingly and slipped out of the room, closing the door behind me. Then I ran down the stairs to the telephone in the hall and dialed Ronnie's number.

From the living room I could hear Dad talking—something about automobile engines—and from the kitchen there came the clank of pans and Mother took something out of the oven. Then Ronnie answered.

"Hello," I said. "This is Lyn."

"Lyn?" He sounded startled. I realized suddenly that it might worry Ronnie for me to call him right on the evening of our date, but it was something that could not be helped.

"Ronnie," I murmured, very conscious of Dale's sharp ears in the next room, "will you do something for me—something important—no questions asked?"

"What?" he asked suspiciously.

"Phone here in an hour," I said, "in exactly one hour, and ask for Susan."

"Susan?" Ronnie repeated. "Why Susan? I don't want to talk to Susan."

There was a sudden rustle in the living room as though

Dale and Dad were getting up to do something. I was filled with panic.

"Please, Ronnie!" I breathed desperately. "Oh, please!" and on that note I hung up and fled upstairs, just as Dale and Dad emerged into the hall.

"Well the deed is done," I panted, flying into my room and shutting the door behind me. "Ronnie's all primed to—" And then I saw Susan.

When you know somebody very well, when you see her every day in school clothes and spend the night with her and see her with her hair up in bobby pins and calamine lotion on her face, even if you know she's pretty, you are inclined to forget it. It must have been that way with Susan, because now, suddenly, seeing her all dressed up for the dance, I caught my breath in awe. She had her hair combed back in a new way, all soft and curly over her shoulders, and her dress was green, just the color of her eyes, and she looked like a princess in a fairy story.

"Will I do?" she asked nervously.

"You look beautiful!" I told her. "Dale won't be able to resist you!" Then I remembered how little time we had before dinner and ran to the closet to get my own dress.

I never dressed for a dance so fast in my life. When Mother called us down to dinner fifteen minutes later, I was ready.

We walked slowly into the dining room with me just a little ahead of Susan, sort of like a herald. I expected gasps of admiration, but all Dale said was, "What took you so long; did you fall down the drain?"

I glanced at Susan to see her reaction to this disgusting remark, but her face was a lovely, serene mask. She merely said, "Hello, Dale."

It was Mother who said, "You look lovely, girls!" But then she added, "Why on earth did you get ready before dinner? You're sure to spill something on yourselves." Which I immediately did, but luckily it was only water.

Dinner seemed to drag on forever. Dale was talking about going bowling that evening with some of the fellows, and Susan was so nervous she could hardly swallow a thing. Just when I thought Ronnie had forsaken us, the phone rang.

"You get it, Dale," I said quickly. Since this was far from my usual reaction to a ringing phone, everyone stared at me in surprise.

"Well, gee whiz!" Dale said, but he got up and went to answer it. He came back two seconds later. "It's some guy for you," he said to Susan, which I considered a good omen as it was the first thing he had said to her all evening.

I waited breathlessly while Susan went to the phone. She came back looking tragic.

"He's sick!" she cried.

"Sick! Who's sick—your father?" Dad was on his feet in an instant. "Do you want me to drive you home?"

"No," Susan explained in a guilty little voice. "It's Fred—Fred Stevens."

"Oh, poor Susan!" I wailed. "Here you are all dressed and ready to go, and you have no date!"

"Huh?" Dale said. "That's funny. I would never have known that was Stevens."

Susan's face turned white. "Oh," she gasped, "you mean you know Fred?"

"Sure," Dale said. "He's in my chemistry class. He sure sounds different on the phone."

I don't know what would have happened at this point if Susan, either from shame or nervousness, had not burst into actual tears. She sank down into her chair and buried her face in her napkin.

"There now, honey," Mother exclaimed, rushing over to her. "We'll work things out some way." And then, just as I had known she would—"Why, Dale can take you!"

"What!" Dale was out of his seat and halfway across the room before we knew where he was going, but Dad stopped him.

"Dale," he said, "come back and sit down. No young man in this house is going to turn his back on a lady in distress. This is one of the things a gentleman just doesn't do."

Dale stopped and came slowly back to his seat. He looked at Dad accusingly.

"Golly," he said, "I didn't think *you'd* do this to me, Dad."

Dad looked a little guilty, but a glance at Susan still sniffling into her napkin reinforced his determination.

"No son of mine," he said decidedly, "is going to walk out on his responsibilities. So march upstairs and put on your good suit and escort this young lady to her dance."

"I don't know where the suit is," Dale said wildly.

"Hanging in your closet," Mother said. "It's all cleaned and pressed."

"But a shirt!" Dale croaked. "I don't have a clean shirt!"

"In your top drawer," Mother told him helpfully, "under your underwear. And, dear," as Dale rose from the table, a trapped expression on his face, "don't forget to polish your shoes. Your feet won't look nearly so large if your shoes are nice and shiny."

Everything was working perfectly. As Susan and I stood in front of the dressing-table mirror in my room, re-pairing our lipstick, I said with a little crow of delight, "It couldn't be better."

"No," Susan agreed, dabbing at her face with a powder puff. But there was no real enthusiasm in her voice.

Later, when Ronnie came to pick us up, I have to admit the evening did not promise to be a particularly pleasant one. Dale was dressed in his good suit and looked quite nice—for Dale, that is—but his expression was grim. He didn't even hold the door for Susan; he just stood there in his usual detestable Dale-like way and scowled at the floor. And Susan, who should have been beaming in triumph, looked simply miserable. I could not help matters much, for my conversation all the way to the school gym was de-voted solely to steering Ronnie away from the subject of the phone call.

When we reached the gym it was even worse. Ronnie is a smooth dancer, and usually dancing with him is just like floating in a dream, but this time I couldn't keep my mind on dancing. I kept looking round the dance floor for Dale and Susan. Whenever I glimpsed them through the crowd I was sorry I had. Dale was staring grimly ahead of him and doing his double-time two-step with Susan held just as far away from him as he could reach, and from the looks of things, Susan was just as miserable as he was.

At last I was too overcome with guilt to be able to stand it any longer. After all, it had been my idea.

"Ronnie," I said, "let's dance over and exchange one

with Dale and Susan. I want to talk to my brother."

Ronnie gave me a surprised look, but he agreeably swung me in Dale's direction. We reached them just as the music stopped. Ronnie asked Susan for the next dance, and as the music started again and they swung off together, Dale gave an unmistakable sigh or relief.

I moved over and took his arm.

"Aren't you going to dance with me?" I asked. "It's the polite thing to do when our partners are dancing together."

"Are you kidding?" He leaned against the wall and put his hands in his pockets.

I was furious. "What's the matter with you?" I asked him angrily. "Here you are with the prettiest girl in school, a girl other boys would give their eyeteeth to take out, and all you do is act as if you hated the whole thing. Why don't you at least pretend you're enjoying yourself and give Susan a good time?"

"Don't be a dope," Dale said. "She wouldn't have a good time with me. She wanted to come with that Stevens guy."

"Oh, for goodness sake!" I began impatiently. "You're just impossi—" I stopped, realizing he was not listening. He was looking across the dance floor at Susan and Ronnie. I followed his gaze and gasped in horror, for there, cutting in on them, his muscles bulging even under the jacket of his suit, was Fred Stevens.

Dale stood there a long moment, staring, and then he turned slowly and looked at me. He had a shocked expression on his face.

"Well," he said, "what was the big idea?"

"Idea?" I said nervously. "What idea?" I couldn't think of a thing to say.

"You know what idea." Now his anger was breaking through. "I thought Fred Stevens was supposed to be sick. There he is, healthy as a horse! You girls thought this whole thing up yourselves. What was the big idea—trying to give yourselves a laugh?"

"What?" Now I was genuinely surprised.

"You wanted to see how dumb I'd look at a dance, didn't you? It would be a real joke to see me dressed up, stumbling around the dance floor, trying to make a hit with the school's most popular girl. It's not enough for the whole family to keep telling me I'm skinny and clumsy and couldn't make the football team—you've got to give yourselves a *real* laugh…"

"But that's not the way it was at all!" I was flabbergasted. I had never seen Dale so angry before. And mixed with the fury, to my amazement, was a terrible strange kind of hurt.

To make matters worse, I looked up and saw Susan and Fred approaching us across the dance floor, with Ronnie trailing naively along.

I tried frantically to signal Susan to stay away, but it was no use. Fred had an iron grip on her arm and seemed determined to escort her politely back to Dale.

"Hi," he said as he reached us, smiling his usual charming football-hero smile. "Good band, isn't it?"

"Yes," I agreed quickly, "Just wonderful."

"Well," he said, "thanks for the dance, Sue."

He turned to go, and for one breathless moment I thought he was going to be out of earshot before Dale erupted. He hesitated, however, and turned back again.

"By the way—congratulations," he said to Dale.

"For what?" Dale asked rudely. He looked about ready to throw something.

"For snagging my date," Fred said, and suddenly he wasn't smiling any longer. "First big dance of the year, and I have to come stag because the one girl I want to take turns me down. Yeah, congratulations." He turned and stalked off without a backward glance.

The silence was awful.

"I guess you're disgusted with me," Susan said at last in a miserable little voice, "and I don't blame you a bit. It was a terrible thing to do. I knew you would never ask me otherwise, and I thought if we had fun tonight you might get to like me better—"

She put her hands over her face and began to cry, but this time there was nothing endearing about her crying—it was dreadful and sniffling and not romantic at all. I guess she'd had about her quota of crying for one night. Anger began to fade from Dale's face and shock returned. It was like seeing a movie backward.

"You turned down Stevens—the captain of the football team! You thought I'd get to like you better?"

"I'm so ashamed," Susan wailed through her hands. "I've never done anything like this before—but you wouldn't ask me yourself. Oh, Dale, I'm so sorry!"

Now, for no reason that I can imagine, both anger and shock were gone from Dale's face.

"Well," he said softly, "well, gee whiz! You wanted me to take you out, huh?" He straightened up and put his shoulders back. Even if he is my brother, in that moment he looked almost handsome. "Well, gee whiz!"

"And I was trying to help," I put in quickly.

Ignoring me completely, Dale put his hand on Susan's shoulder. It was a moment in which, being Dale, he should have said something perfectly detestable. Instead, he said, "Why don't you go powder your nose or something, and come back, and we'll dance. I—I'd really like to dance."

Susan lowered her hands and smiled at Dale. Her eyes were red and watery and her face splotchy and I had never seen her look so dreadful. No one would ever guess she was supposed to be a pretty girl.

"Sue," Dale said gruffly, "you look really nice tonight."

I turned to Ronnie, who was standing there, not understanding a thing that was happening.

"Come on," I said, "let's dance." Because all of a sudden I felt that Dale might handle everything pretty well. All of a sudden I felt as though—maybe—a boy's sister doesn't know him at all.

(written at the age of 21)

☆　☆　☆　☆　☆　☆　☆　☆　☆　☆　☆　☆　☆　☆

Why did I write "Detestable Dale"? I'm trying to remember. I wrote it at age 21, when I was the mother of my first baby. My young husband had just graduated from college and entered the military, and I was churning out story after story in an effort to supplement his meager income.

For that reason, the stories I wrote at that time are inclined to run together in my memory, and I can't always recall the circumstances behind the writing of each one. However, I can guess what might have triggered this one. That was the year that my brother was a senior in high school, and suddenly, to my astonishment, had turned into a "ladies' man." Although I had never considered my brother Bill "detestable," as Lynn does Dale, I had never imagined that he was going to become a heart-breaker. After all, he was my brother!

Little things like that can spark the idea for a story. Then the writer's creativity takes over and develops it as fiction.

April

My sister's name is April. She was born in the spring. Mother says it was the first real day of spring when the air was suddenly warm and soft and fresh and dandelions popped out on the lawn and the first group of birds invaded the birdbath in the backyard. Mother isn't usually the romantic type, but when she heard the birds and felt springtime pouring in the open window she completely forgot the baby was to be named Martha Dunning after an aunt.

She said, "Her name is April."

So when I came along a year later, the Martha Dunning name was still lying around, waiting to be used. I was born in the hottest part of August, so there was no inspiration for anything else.

I've often wondered whether, if things had been different—if I had been the springtime baby and April had come in dead summer and been Martha Dunning—maybe we would have been different people too. I've wondered how much being named April had to do with making April look like springtime. Because she does. Even when we were very little, people would look at April with her soft, light hair shining silver over her shoulders and her eyes a dark, dark blue, almost a purple blueness, and they'd smile. As she grew older the loveliness did not fade the way it does with so many pretty children. If anything, she grew more beautiful each day.

Sometimes I would catch Mother and Daddy looking at her and then glancing at each other and shaking their heads as though to ask, "How in the world did we—two quite average people—ever produce anything like this!" And aside from being exquisite to look at, April is sweet. It is a gentle, childlike sweetness that makes her like and trust everybody, and when she was little, Mother and Daddy were fiercely protective of her. Although she was the older, I always felt as though she were my younger sister, and in all our games I was the one who led and made the rules. She was a year ahead of me in school, but it was I who taught her to read, carefully pointing out the letters and pronouncing the words.

"Oh, Martha," April would sigh, staring at the page in bewilderment, "I'll never be able to do it. All those letters making words and the words making sense—how do you ever remember what they all are! I'm so dumb!"

"No," I would say quickly, "you're not dumb, April. You'll learn. It just takes time."

"But look at you!" April would exclaim. "You've been able to read practically since you were a baby!"

Which was true. I loved books with a passionate devotion, and the challenge of reading had never held any terrors for me.

"Oh, some people are good at some things, and some at others." I would say reassuringly. "Come on and try again."

At last she did learn to read, at least well enough to get by, but she never liked it. I don't believe I have ever seen April pick up a book for pleasure. And then came a worse step—multiplication tables—and then long division and fractions and algebra, and finally civics and biology and chemistry. Through them all, April struggled earnestly, and I spent hours with her at home, and finally when our report cards came out, she would produce D's and C's, and Mother and Daddy would always say, "Well, that's fine, dear."

And to my straight A's they would say, "That's fine dear," in exactly the same tone of voice. And April would smile with such radiant relief that they would kiss her impulsively. Because, after all, she did try so hard and was so beautiful.

Our house was a good-sized one and April and I each had her own room. April's room was the smaller, but it had a window overlooking the backyard garden and in summer it always smelled of flowers and freshly cut grass. It was done in pink and with white fluffy curtains at the windows and a dressing table with a ruffle around it covered with pink rosebuds. My room was yellow and brown with a chocolate rug and sunny curtains and several rows of bookshelves and a large desk. The rooms were as different as we were, but they were both nice in their own ways.

"Your room looks so comfortable in winter," April would say, wandering in to toss herself across the foot of the bed where I lay reading. "I think it's the yellow—it seems so warm and friendly."

"Well, you can spend the winter with me," I would answer, "and I'll come visit your room in the spring."

Then we would both laugh, for we knew how hopeless our sharing a room would be—like trying to mix orange sherbet with mashed potatoes.

I liked my room. It suited me, and there was plenty

of room for the books I loved so much and for my desk, which never would have fitted into April's room. Even so, sometimes I would pass her door and glance in and see the fluff of curtains and the rosebud dressing table, and I would wonder what it would be like to have such a dainty room and to fit in it as perfectly as April did.

We both had our boyfriends. April, of course, had admirers in droves from the time she started kindergarten, and by the time she reached high school she never had a choice of less that three or four invitations to the school dances. I went to the dances too, although my admirers seemed to consist of only one boy at a time. I was never actually jealous, because April whisked back and forth from one boy to another so gaily that it made it all seem like a game.

Until the arrival of Jeff Reigle.

Jeff was much older than the boys we were used to dating. We never would have known him at all if Daddy had not been introduced to him at the Rotary Club. He was a fine young man, Daddy told us, in business for himself, and Daddy had invited him over for dinner.

"April's a senior now—eighteen years old," he told us. "It's time she met somebody besides the high school crowd."

"How old is *he?*" we asked in amazement. Daddy had always been strict about our dating boys our own age.

"Oh, twenty-five or twenty-six," Daddy said casually.

April and I were stunned. "Ancient!" we whispered to each other.

But when Jeff arrived he was not ancient at all. Nor was he handsome. He was tall and sturdy with a square, stubborn chin, and he was wearing a slightly surly expression, as though he were not in the least happy about being dragged to meet a couple of high school girls. But there was something about him—a strength and maturity—that was very attractive.

"—my daughters…" Daddy was saying, "April and Martha Dunning."

Jeff nodded politely at April and then at me, and then his eyes shifted back to April, and the sullen expression left his face. Instead there came into his eyes the look that boys always got when they looked at April. I had never minded before, but suddenly I felt a sudden heaviness in the pit of my stomach.

He said, "How do you do, Martha Dunning…April…" and his voice lingered on the "April" as though surprised at how well the name fitted the girl. I thought what a perfectly ghastly name Martha Dunning was in comparison.

April smiled. Her smile is wonderful, like a flood of sunlight. She smiles at everybody, but anyone on the receiving end is always absolutely sure that she has been waiting her whole lifetime just to smile at him.

I don't remember exactly what we talked about that evening. I know that Jeff was wonderfully polite; he divided his attention equally between us. He asked me if I liked sports and where I wanted to go to college and what books I read. He even seemed to be interested in my answers, but then his eyes would wander back to April.

After Jeff left and April and I were upstairs getting ready for bed, I tried to think of some way to bring the conversation around to Jeff, but I did not have to because April mentioned him herself.

"He's nice, isn't he?" she said dreamily. "Jeff Reigle, I mean."

"Yes." I glanced sideways at her, standing in front of my mirror, brushing her hair.

"He asked me for a date when he was saying good-night," she said. "It's for this Friday. I think it should be fun, don't you?"

I nodded, feeling my throat tighten.

"You have a date Friday night too, don't you, Martha?"

"Yes," I said. "I do." It was with Timmy Kantor, one of the boys in my class. Timmy was pleasant and I had been looking forward to the evening, but now suddenly I didn't think I could bear to have Friday come.

As it turned out, Timmy arrived early, so I never got to see Jeff. We got home around eleven-thirty, and I said a hurried goodnight and went upstairs. April wasn't home yet. I went to my room and set my hair and got ready for bed and tried to settle down to read, but I could not concentrate. It was almost one o'clock before I heard the tap of April's feet in the hall.

She hesitated by my door, saw the light, and came in.

She was wearing a green dress that swished about her like spring breezes and her hair was rippling silver across her shoulders. She smiled at me, and I knew how she must have looked to Jeff.

I said, "Hi. Did you have a nice time?"

"Oh, yes," breathed April. "It was marvelous! We had dinner on the terrace of the San Carlos Hotel. There was dancing, and there's nothing but sky over you up there and when you look down off the edge, you can see lights all the way down to the river."

"What's Jeff like?" I asked, trying to keep my voice casual.

"Jeff? Oh, Martha!" and her voice was singing in a way I never had heard before, "Martha, he's wonderful! He's not like anybody I've ever known! He treated me like something precious … as if I was going to break any minute … and he thinks I'm beautiful!'"

She said it with such wonder and joy that I was able to keep my resentment out of my voice.

"Of course he does" I said. "Because you are. You're innocent and sweet and springtime. You're"—I managed to smile—"you're *April*."

April smiled too, not really understanding.

"Well, of course, I'm April," she said. "And you're Martha Dunning. And you must have had quite an evening yourself to be talking like such a nut! Good night."

After she was gone I lay there for a long time, thinking. April was beautiful and unspoiled, but was that really enough? Oh, for the high school boys, yes. But Jeff Reigle was a grown man, his school days far behind him, established in his own business, used to adult companionship. What really did he and April have to talk about? April was never tongue-tied—she could chatter gaily along about school and parties and movie stars—but surely after a while this could become boring to a man like Jeff. I, on the other hand, had read so much; I had opinions on so many things that school boys shrugged off as silly, but things a man might respond to and find interesting.

It wouldn't hurt to try anyway, I thought defensively. After all, April had so many boys in love with her, and Jeff Reigle was the first man I'd ever felt this way about. If I could get him interested in me intellectually, surely that wouldn't hurt April …

I don't know, thinking back on it, if my plan would have worked. Sometimes I think it would have; other times I don't. There were occasions, I know, there in the beginning before their love was established and final, when Jeff did seem a little bored with April's chatter. I tried to make the most of those opportunities. I would ask Jeff something about a book we'd both read—about art or politics or philosophy—something that would leave April out of the conversation or would cause her to make some remark that showed her ignorance. And Jeff would be interested. He liked stimulating conversation, and he would turn to me eagerly.

April didn't know what was going on. She is never suspicious of anyone, least of all me.

Mother, however, is not gullible. She drew me aside one day and said quietly, "Martha Dunning, I know what you are doing, or trying to do, and I don't want to see any more of it."

"What do you mean?" I asked, a little frightened by Mother's tone of voice.

"Jeff is April's beau," she said decidedly. "He is right for April; he is old enough and strong enough to take care of her the way your father and I have always done. I don't want you spoiling things for them, Martha Dunning."

"Mother!" I gasped in amazement. "You sound as though you want them to get married!"

"Well," Mother said thoughtfully, "Jeff would make April a good husband."

At first I was too stunned to reply. Finally I said, "What about me? Don't you care about my having a good husband too?"

"Oh, for goodness sake," Mother said impatiently. "You just think you care for Jeff because he's the first eligible mature man that you've had a chance to know. You'll find somebody at college or afterward. You have all the time in the world, Martha Dunning."

And that, of course, was the end of my plan.

Jeff and April were married that spring right after April's graduation. The wedding was held in the little church two blocks from our home, and we had the reception in our garden. People said it was the loveliest event they could remember. April looked like an angel drifting down the aisle in her wedding gown with her hair shimmering in the sunlight that flowed through the stained glass windows, and afterward when she threw back her veil and lifted her radiant face to Jeff's, there wasn't a person in the church who did not catch his breath.

At the reception I glanced across the lawn at Mother and Daddy. They were standing very close together, hand in hand, watching April with a glow on their faces that nearly matched her own. Standing there in my pink gown, which I knew I'd never wear again, I thought resentfully, why did April have to insist on her maid of honor wearing pink when she knew that yellow was my best color? I felt a surge of bitterness toward April for being so beautiful and toward Jeff for marrying her, and toward Mother and Daddy for loving her so much. It was an ugly feeling. I knew that, and I was ashamed of it, but I could not drive it away.

There was one moment during the reception when I almost moved past it. It was when April flew up to me, her face glowing, and impulsively seized my hands and said in that soft, sweet way of hers, "Oh, Martha, I only hope you're as happy on your wedding day as I am now!"

I squeezed her hands and said, "You deserve to be happy, honey." But, then, as she turned away, the envy returned in a vicious surge because I saw Mother standing by the buffet table, beaming at her.

During the next year, it was hard to believe that April was now Mrs. Jeffery Reigle. She and Jeff had an apartment of their own, but it was only a block away, and April was always popping in and out of our house almost as though she still lived there. She would arrive in the morning after Jeff left for work and sit in the kitchen chatting with Mother, or she would dash in for lunch, or she would stop by on her way to the grocery store to see if one of us wanted to go along. I was surprised at the delight she took in the apartment. At home she never had shown much liking for domestic things, but now with her own four rooms to decorate and care for she was like a child with a new toy. Mother spent a good deal of each day over at the apartment, teaching her how to do things—how to cook Jeff's favorite dishes and how to wax a wooden floor, and what to do when the toilet was stopping up or the refrigerator wouldn't defrost. She and April worked together for a full week making curtains, and they would phone each other to swap recipes and talk "woman talk". It was as though, suddenly, April and Mother were on one step of a ladder and I was alone on another, and I hated it.

"You know," I said one day at dinner, "I think I'll move into April's old room. I've always liked it, and it would be nice to have a window facing out over the garden."

Mother said, "Martha, that's ridiculous! Where in the

world would you put all your books and your desk if you moved into April's little room?"

"I'll leave them in my old room," I said. "I can always go there and get anything I need or work at my desk in there. I'll have April's room as a bedroom and my old room as a kind of study."

"Oh, no, you won't!" Mother exclaimed. "Two rooms, indeed! One of those rooms is going to be a guest room, Martha Dunning. We've never had a guest room, and I've always longed for one. You will stay in your own nice room, just as you always have."

"You'll be going away to college next year anyway," Daddy added.

"Going to college?" I repeated. I felt a wave of laughter welling up within me. For once I was going to be the center of as much astonishment, confusion and incredulous delight as April. I hesitated, wondering if this was the time to tell them. Perhaps it wasn't, but I knew I could not hold my secret any longer.

"I'm not going to college next fall," I announced triumphantly. "I'm going to be married!"

"What!"

Never in my wildest dreams had I imagined the amazement that covered their faces. I was so happy I could hardly continue.

"Yes," I said. "To Timmy. He asked me several weeks ago, but I was waiting to surprise you. His dad has promised him a job in his clothing store after graduation. We're going to get an apartment, maybe in the same building with April and Jeff, and fix it all up and"—I hesitated, realizing that the surprise on their faces had given way to a look that was far from the delight I had anticipated—"and everything," I continued lamely.

"You certainly are not!" Daddy said as soon as I stopped talking. "Throw over college and marry a shirt salesman the minute you get out of high school? That's the craziest thing I ever heard."

I felt my face growing hot with anger.

"You didn't say that when April wanted to get married! In fact, you did everything you possibly could to marry her off to Jeff. And she wasn't very much older than I'll be when I graduate!"

"That was different," Mother said. "Now, you just forget this getting married business, Martha Dunning, and buckle down to your studies and get yourself ready for the college entrance exams."

That was all they would say. They refused to discuss it anymore. Timmy and I toyed with the idea of eloping, but we were both slightly under age, and we knew our parents could have the marriage annulled as soon as they located us. Besides, when I thought about getting married I visualized a lovely church wedding with a reception in our garden, just like April's, with Mother and Daddy beaming proudly and people surging all over the place, gasping and exclaiming about what a beautiful (well, at least "attractive") bride I was. And, then, the apartment with Mother making a grand fuss over how cute it was and helping me fix it up to make it even cuter. Somehow, when my parents drained all the excitement from the idea, my enthusiasm for Timmy began to wane as well. By springtime we weren't even going steady any longer, and we both attended the Prom with different people.

And then it was June and time for my graduation. I was valedictorian of our class and had a speech to make at Commencement. Mother and Daddy seemed pleased about that, but as it turned out, even this day of glory was not fully my own. April chose that time to announce that she was going to have a baby.

"I know I should have told you sooner," she said happily, "but I thought it would be just perfect to wait and tell you tonight so the news would be a kind of special graduation present for Martha Dunning. It's due in October. Isn't this marvelous!"

"Yes," I agreed. "Marvelous."

I knew in my heart that what April was saying was true. She had saved the news to tell tonight only because she thought I would be pleased to have it for part or my graduation excitement. Her joy was pure and complete, and I knew she expected mine to be as well, but it was not. Somehow the evening no longer was mine—it was April's. When I rose that night to give my speech, I looked out over the audience and saw my family sitting there, watching me, but even as I spoke I saw Mother turn and glance sideways at April as though wondering how she felt. And afterward, when I was preparing for bed and passed Mother's and Daddy's bedroom on the way to the bathroom I heard them talking. It was not about my speech, or how impressive I had looked in my cap and gown, or how proud they were of my honors.

"A baby!" Mother was saying. "Why she doesn't know the first thing about babies! How will she manage—think of the responsibility—"

"There, now," Daddy said reassuringly. "It'll work out.

We'll be here to help her, just as we've always been. It'll be sort of nice having a baby in the family again, won't it? April's baby?"

"Yes," Mother admitted somewhat reluctantly. "It will be."

I went on into the bathroom and brushed my teeth so hard that my gums bled. When I passed their door again, I did not stop to say good night; I went straight to my room and shut the door and lay there on the bed, hating April with all my might. Later there were footsteps in the hall and a light tap at my door, but I did not answer. I knew it was Mother, and I did not want to talk to her. After a few moments the footsteps went away.

That was the longest, slowest summer I can remember. Mother spent most of her time at April's apartment, cleaning and cooking and making sure that April didn't do anything stressful. And April, to my disgust, had never looked lovelier, even wearing baggy maternity tops and skirts with elastic waistbands.

"Martha," she said to me once, "I may never have been good in school, but I do think I'll do a good job having a baby."

"Yes," I said shortly, "you undoubtedly will."

There was no gentleness in my voice and April looked at me in surprise. Then she smiled.

"Honestly," she said, "I think you've suffered through this pregnancy much more than I have. Martha Dunning, I've never seen you as snappish as you've been lately. Are you worried about me, honey? Please, don't be. I'm just fine, really."

"No," I said truthfully, "I'm not worried about you at all."

September arrived, and with it the start of college. Mother did not go with me to buy my college wardrobe; she just had Daddy write me a check with the amount left open and told me to buy anything I thought I would need. Any other time the idea of such independence would have filled me with delight, but now as I drove into town I kept thinking about Mother and April, rushing about from shop to shop together, buying things for the baby. At least, I thought, Mother might have shown enough interest to want to go with me.

I shopped all day and came home with a nice assortment of clothes. Mother nodded when she saw them and said I had good taste and had found excellent values, and April exclaimed over my sexy new evening gown and laughed about how wonderful it would be to be able to fit into something like that again. But when they got out a bunch of little nightgowns they were embroidering with daisies and began to discuss whether to use pink or blue for the centers of the flowers, I went alone to carry the clothes up to my room and put them away.

The first weeks of college were stimulating, and I would have really enjoyed them if I had been able to relax and forget about April and all the excitement that was going on at home without me. April's baby was due the twelfth of October, and I wrote Mother that I had reservations home the afternoon of the eleventh.

"I know you'll need me," I wrote, "to help around the house and take care of April's apartment while she's in the hospital and give you both a hand with the baby when she gets it home. I can use all my semester cuts, plus the weekend, and spend a full week there."

I waited a week for what I thought would be Mother's grateful reply, but when it came it was highly unenthusiastic.

"We appreciate your wanting to help," she wrote, "but, truly, dear, the fewer people that are here the less confusion there will be. Besides, Jeff is going to be staying with us while April is in the hospital. Then April and Jeff and the baby will all be staying here until April gets her strength back and the baby is sleeping through the night, so your room is going to be in use. Study hard and have a good time at college, and we will telegraph you as soon as the baby arrives."

As I read that letter I felt more left out and unwanted than I ever had before, and then more angry. There was nothing to be done but sit and wait for the telegram.

The twelfth came, and the thirteenth, and the fourteenth. A week passed, and then another. And no telegram.

I burst forth with my bitterness to my roommate.

"They promised!" I raged. "They gave their word they'd telegraph me immediately!"

"Oh, don't get so upset about it," my roommate said soothingly. "After all, there's probably so much confusion they forgot about that. Why don't *you* phone *them*?"

I did phone that night. I meant it to be a short call. I meant to ask in a quiet, injured voice whether I had a niece or a nephew. Instead, when I heard Mother's voice on the other end of the line, the anger that had been pent up in me for so long burst over and I found myself saying things I could never have imagined saying.

"You didn't telegraph!" I stormed. "You didn't even bother to think I might be wondering what was going on.

You were so wrapped up in your precious April! All my life it's been 'April, April, April.' April gets the garden room! April's allowed to get married! April gets any little thing she wants, always! Well, I'm sick and tired of it. I may not be as pretty as April, but I'm your daughter too. I'm sick of April—sick to death of her—and I hope her baby turned out to be a two-headed monster!"

I clamped the receiver down on the hook and stood there in the booth, shaking with fury, and then suddenly the full horror of what I had done—of what I had said—swept over me. I leaned back against the wall of the booth and heard the words again, rasping in my ears. "I'm sick to death of April—I hope her baby—"

"No," I whispered. "Oh, no. I didn't mean that, Mother. I didn't mean that at all!"

But the receiver was back on the hook, and Mother was hundreds of miles away.

I turned and went up to my dorm room, knowing that any love my parents had ever had for me would be gone after this, and I couldn't blame them. This I could not blame on April. Only on myself.

I went to class the next morning just as I always did, though I can't pretend that I listened carefully to the lectures. And afterward, having skipped breakfast, I walked over to the cafeteria and forced myself to eat a decent lunch before going back to the dorm to study. I walked to the dormitory, still alone, for my roommate had an afternoon lab, and opened the door to our room.

There, sitting in the chair by the window, was Mother.

"Mother!" I gasped. "What are you doing here! Is something the matter? Is—" And suddenly my knees were so weak that I could not stand. I stumbled forward and sat down on the end of the bed. "It's April," I whispered. "April—the baby—something awful's happened."

Terror shot through me, sharp and icy, with a pain so great that I could hardly breathe. My stomach lurched and I thought, I'm going to be sick—all that lunch I ate—and I reached out my hand crazily for the bedside table, for something to hold onto, but the table was farther away than I thought and I could not reach it. The whole room was a million miles away—the chair—the desk—even Mother, and all I could see was April's face dancing before my eyes. I could hear her laughter, bright and careless, filling the room with the sound of springtime and see her turn to me with that puzzled expression in her eyes, the way she did when she could not understand something and wanted me to explain it.

"April," I whispered. "The baby is …"

Suddenly Mother was beside me on the bed with her arms tight around me.

"No, Martha," she was saying over and over again. "Honey, no. Nothing's the matter with April. I'm sorry I frightened you. I didn't realize—" She was shaking me, trying to get me to listen to her. "Martha, listen, dear— April's all right. The baby's overdue, that's all. It very often happens with first babies. Why, when I left last night, April was at a baby shower over at Nancy's house."

Slowly her words penetrated and the world began to fall back into place.

"She's all right?" I repeated. "And the baby—it hasn't even been born yet?"

"No," Mother said. "At least, it hadn't been when I left.

April had started to have a few back pains, that's all."

I stared at her. "Then what are you doing here! You left April when her baby's due any minute?"

Mother's arms were still around me. "April's all right," she said quietly. "She's got Jeff. I think my other daughter is the one who needs me right now."

I don't know exactly when I started to cry, but now I was conscious of the tears streaming down my cheeks. I buried my face against Mother's shoulder and let them come, and it was as though all the tension and resentment and jealousy that had built up for so long were pouring out with the tears. I cried for a long time, and after I grew quiet Mother began to talk.

"I didn't know," she said. "Until you called last night, I didn't have any idea how you felt about April. I took it for granted you understood. You're so smart, Martha Dunning—why, sometimes when you came to us with a poem you'd written or a book you wanted to discuss, Daddy and I would look at each other in amazement—we just couldn't believe that a child of ours could have a mind like yours. So I assumed that you understood things when you obviously didn't.

"Do you remember the Christmas we gave you the Mickey Mouse watch?"

"No," I said hesitantly. And, then, "Yes." For suddenly I did remember. I had not thought of it in years, but out of the past came the memory of that wondrous moment when I pulled aside the tissue paper and saw the watch—a real one with hands that moved. "I was six years old."

"Yes." Mother nodded. "April didn't get a watch. Do you remember why?"

"She couldn't tell time," I said immediately, "and I could."

"Yes," Mother said again. "Poor April, in the second grade, and she still couldn't tell time. I think we gave her a baby doll that Christmas. But it wasn't because we loved you better that we gave you the better gift—it was because the watch was right for you and it wasn't right for April.

"No two children," she continued slowly, "are the same. The things that are good for one may not be right for another, and parents have to decide what is best for each. Sometimes they are wrong, but at least they have to try.

"When April wanted to marry Jeff, it seemed like a good thing. We've always known April would marry early (can you imagine her trying to go to college or have a career?) and we were glad for her husband to be a mature, responsible man who would take care of her, rather than one of the boys her own age who could hardly take care of himself. Jeff had a business right there in town so we knew April would be close enough for us to help out with any problems, just as we've always done, and she could have her pretty apartment and her babies, which are all April needs to make her happy. But you, honey—why, you need more than that! You need a chance to use your mind, to see and do things by yourself, to meet young men with education and ambition! You'd go crazy with a husband who sold shirts in a men's store! You'd be bored to death with nothing to do but hem curtains and change babies. Not," she added quickly, "that you won't want babies, but you must have a chance at something else first."

She stopped and drew back a little so she could see my face.

"It had nothing to do with loving April more. Or you more. Can you see that, Martha Dunning?"

I felt so ashamed of myself I could hardly speak.

"Yes," I said. "I can."

Mother was starting to say something more when there was a quick rap at the door and one of the girls stuck her head in.

"Martha?" she said. "Is your mother in the dorm? There's a long distance call for her at the desk."

Mother practically flew down the hall to the telephone booth. It was a full five minutes later that she emerged, triumphant.

"April's baby has come!"she exclaimed. "It's a healthy, seven pound, six ounce girl! April's fine, the labor was amazingly quick, and the delivery was an easy one. Everything's perfect!"

Her face was aglow with happiness, the same happiness she would feel, someday in the future, at the birth of *my* baby. And looking at her I felt joy flowing through me—a mixture of wonder and pride and relief—and my own love for April, which I had pushed from me for so long, rose up within me.

"Oh!" I whispered. "I'm so glad. A girl! I wonder what they will name her!"

"Well," Mother said, "that was Jeff on the phone. He says that if it's all right with you, April wants to name her baby Martha Dunning. She says she's always thought it was the most beautiful name she'd ever heard."

(written at the age of 23)

☆ ☆ ☆ ☆ ☆ ☆ ☆ ☆ ☆ ☆ ☆ ☆ ☆ ☆

In 1957, the fiction editor at *Seventeen Magazine* wrote asking if I might possibly have a story on file about the relationship between two sisters. I didn't but I agreed to write one.

Back in my grammar-school days, I had ridden the school bus with a girl named Martha Dunning. "Dunning" wasn't her last name; it went with the "Martha." People called her Martha Dunning when they spoke to her. I was horrified by the idea of being known by such a mouthful, and once I timidly asked her how she felt about it. She told me it was a family name and she was used to it, and then added, after a short pause, "You should hear what our folks named my sister."

I didn't have the nerve to ask her, and I'd wondered about it ever since. Was the sister's name longer or shorter? Prettier or uglier? The question had hung dormant in the back of my mind for over twelve years. Now it came popping out to give me a jump-off point for a story.

Time To Find Out

I received a letter from Ralph yesterday, postmarked Germany, saying he'll be home in a couple of weeks. "Home" for Ralph means Trenton, New Jersey, but he said, "I'll be down to see you some weekend soon," so I guess he will. Duke University is only a day's drive from Trenton, and for a boy who has spent yesterday on the other side of the ocean, a day's drive isn't anything at all.

I read the letter to Anna, who was stretched out on the other bed, sorting her history notes.

"I wonder if he's changed much," I said. "It's been so long, and it's hard to tell in letters."

"Probably," said Anna. "But then you have too, of course." She riffled through a pile of note cards and added casually, a little too casually, "I wonder what he hears from Vietti."

"I wonder too," I said. *Vietti.* I thought, if it weren't for Vietti I might be married to Ralph now. I'd be sitting here wondering how he's changed, and I'd be talking about my husband!

But I couldn't say that to Anna. I just said, "I wonder too," and folded the letter and put it in my top bureau drawer.

It's not that I was ever in love with Vietti myself. I

suppose I could have been if things had been different, but as it was, I was Ralph's girl, and nobody could be Ralph's girl and be in love with somebody else at the same time. Ralph took all the time and energy and emotion it was possible to spend on anybody. I liked Vietti—no one could help liking him—but I was never in love with him.

Anna was—just three years ago. It started like this.

She showed me his picture in English class one morning. It was a horrible snapshot, as most of Anna's efforts at photography were inclined to be. All I could tell was that the person in it was a boy in uniform with his arms crossed and a hat pulled down over his eyes.

Anna beamed proudly.

"He's darling," she informed me. I was sure he must be. Anna didn't have to waste her time on boys who weren't.

"Where did you meet him?" I asked.

"At the beach this past Sunday. Are you sure you don't know him? He's in the same barracks as Ralph."

"No," I said. "Ralph never introduces me to any of the other boys if he can help it. Did he ask you for a date?"

"No," Anna said. "Not yet. But he knows my name."

I glanced at her quickly and smiled despite myself. She was wearing a white turtleneck sweater and a neat black skirt. Her eyes were cool and green, and when she saw me looking at her, she raised one eyebrow and smiled back.

I thought, Poor guy! Whoever he is, he's lost already!

I was very pleased. Now that I belonged securely to Ralph, there was nothing I enjoyed more than seeing a new boy fall for Anna.

But, oddly enough, nothing happened. The week passed, and the weekend came again, and Anna turned down the usual offering of assorted dates with the local high school boys, but Vietti never called her. What surprised me most was that she worried about that. I had never seen Anna worried about a boy before, and I couldn't understand it.

"What does it matter, whether he calls or not?" I asked her. "You certainly don't need to worry about sitting home on weekend nights."

"But this is different."

"Why is it different?" I insisted. "You hardly know him."

"But it is different," she said impatiently. "He's different. He's—oh, I can't explain it. You've got to meet him to understand."

Anna was in love. It was as simple as that. After meeting a boy one time and being with him for a couple of hours in a crowd on the beach, Anna was in love.

Then I met him, and I saw why.

None of the boys at the Air Force Training School had cars, and they hated it. They complained about the food and the drills and the laundry, but those would have been endurable if only they had been allowed to have their cars. Ralph and I walked and took buses, and once in a great while I got the family car and Ralph paid for the gas. It was on one of those great occasions that I met Vietti.

Ralph introduced us regretfully.

"This is Tony Vietti," he said. "I told him we'd give him a ride uptown. This is Janie." His voice took on a note of emphasis. "She's *my* girlfriend."

Vietti wasn't handsome. I was surprised, because Anna always went with handsome boys. He was tall and lean, with a pleasant monkey face and bright red hair and dark eyes. There was nothing astonishing about him, nothing to pluck at the heartstrings or make a girl pick him out of a crowd and remember him afterward.

And then, suddenly, he smiled, and I knew why Anna loved him. If Ralph hadn't been there with his arm possessively around my shoulders and his dog tags swinging in my face, I might have fallen a little in love with him myself.

"Hello," I said. "Hop in."

Ralph came around and got into the driver's seat, and Vietti got in back.

"Where are you from?" I asked as Ralph started the engine. It was the stock question everyone asked the boys.

"Chicago." His voice croaked oddly, and I glanced back at him. I had never seen anybody look so homesick in my whole life.

I said, "I went to Chicago once with my parents. My dad was attending a convention there."

I thought back, desperately trying to remember what Chicago had been like. It all blurred into stockyards and high buildings and museums and a cold gust of wind every time a door was opened. As a city I couldn't really remember it at all.

"Isn't it great?" Vietti exclaimed eager. "There's no place like it—no place in the world."

All the way from the base into town we discussed the merits of Chicago. At last Ralph pulled the car over to the curb and stopped it, leaving the motor running.

"Okay," he said gruffly. "Is this far enough up town to drop you off, feller?"

"Yes," said Vietti. "Sure. Thanks a million."

He looked at me. "Thanks," he repeated. "I'm sure glad to have met you."

He scrambled out of the car, straightened out his long legs, and started off along the sidewalk. He was walking slowly, aimlessly. He looked very young and very much alone.

Ralph stepped on the gas, and the car swung out into the street. We drove along in silence.

"You might have asked him to come with us," I said at last. "He seemed so kind of lost."

"Yeah," Ralph said caustically. "I'm sure that you'd have liked that. I guess you've both got a lot in common, having been to Chicago and all. I guess maybe you'd like to go out with Vietti instead of me, wouldn't you?"

He was scowling, his lower lip thrust forward and his hands clenched on the wheel.

"No," I said softly, "I don't want to go out with him." I reached out my hand and touched Ralph's hair, letting my fingers trail across the side of his face, and I felt his muscles tighten in response. I was filled with a tremendous sense of power.

This is what Anna does to boys, I thought with delight, and I do it to Ralph.

I leaned my head back against his shoulder.

"I'm just interested in Vietti," I said, "because a good friend of mine met him a couple of weeks ago. She thought he was going to call her, and then he didn't."

"Oh." Ralph's relief was evident.

"I don't suppose," I continued, "that you could fix it up for her, could you?"

"Well," Ralph said without much enthusiasm, "I don't know. I don't think I've ever known him to go out with a girl. He's probably got a girl back home, or he's just not interested."

I said, "He seems so lonely, Ralph, and my friend is awfully nice. Give it a try anyway, won't you, please?"

Ralph said, "Sure, honey, I'll give it a try." He reached down and put his hand over mine. "Look," he said awkwardly, "I'm sorry about the way I just acted. I don't mean to get jealous. It's just—well, home's so far away and you're all I've got here. I—I need you." His voice sounded so young and unsure that I felt a surge of warmth flood through me. It was the first time anyone had ever seemed really to need me. I squeezed his hand and leaned my head back against his shoulder again, and I wondered if anyone, ever, had been so completely happy.

At school the next day I told Anna I had met Vietti.

"What did you think of him?" she asked eagerly.

"Adorable," I admitted, "just as you said. But he's not the least bit handsome. It must be his smile."

"Yes," Anna agreed, "it's his smile."

For as long as I could remember, Anna had been getting me dates. It wasn't always directly; it was simply that wherever Anna went, boys congregated, and I, as Anna's best friend, came in for my share. She didn't have to make any special effort and roll her hair at night and powder her nose every two minutes the way most of us girls did. She had merely to walk across the room or glance sideways and laugh, and whether it was on a beach or in a classroom or at a football game, every boy within a hundred yards would find some excuse to drift in her direction. Since only one boy could date Anna in a single evening, the others would shrug philosophically and take me instead.

That is, all except Ralph. Ralph had never looked twice at Anna. Ralph was the only boy who had ever been—without question—mine from the very beginning.

Now I smiled and said, "I've asked Ralph to fix it up for you." After the dozens of dates she had given me, I was going to give Anna the one boy she couldn't get. I was going to give her Vietti.

Ralph managed it. He told me on the phone, "He's coming, but he wouldn't be if he wasn't so bored with sitting in the barracks every night. He's not very keen on the idea. I predict it's going to be one dead evening."

He was wrong.

The boys picked us both up at my house. Anna and I looked nice—we were sure of that because we had spent an hour in front of the mirror preparing ourselves—but the moment the boys walked in, Anna stopped looking nice and began to look beautiful. She looked at Vietti, and he looked at her; and there was a warmth and a glow and a loveliness about her that I had never seen before.

"Hello," she said. "Do you remember me?"

"Yes," said Vietti. "Yes. Sure. Of course I do."

I thought, she looks beautiful! I wonder if I look that beautiful when I look at Ralph. I rather doubted that I did and yet I was beginning to think I was in love with Ralph. It was hard to understand.

"Come on," I said, slipping my arm through his. "Let's go."

We took the bus. It was crowded and we had to stand up all the way, laughing and bumping against each other as it lurched to a stop at every corner and tumbling helplessly into people's laps when it started. We had to walk several blocks from the bus stop to the movie theater, and even the walk was fun. It was that kind of night.

The rest of the evening passed too swiftly. I sat through

the movie with Ralph's arm around me and a box of popcorn in my lap and Vietti on the other side of me. Every once in a while, Vietti would lean over and whisper something to Anna, and she would laugh, and he would laugh with her. They were still laughing together when we left the theater, easily and happily as though they had known each other forever.

I glanced up at Ralph. "You were wrong," I whispered, but he pretended not to hear.

When we reached my house, where Anna was to spend the night, we split forces. Ralph drew me around to the back yard where we sat in the hammock for a while.

We had been talking idly, about nothing really, when suddenly he said, "I love you." He put his arms around me when he said it, and the words sounded strange and wonderful, the way I had always imagined they must sound when a boy said them.

I said, "Ralph—" I wanted to say, "I love you too," but the words stuck in my throat, and for some reason I was afraid to say them. Maybe because I had never said them before.

He tightened his arms and said, "You'll miss me, won't you?"

"Miss you!" I was startled. "What do you mean, miss you?"

"Well, gee," he said. "Our training will be over in another month. We're not going to be here forever, you know. We'll probably be headed overseas after this."

My heart fell, and I felt a hollowness inside me so great that I thought for a moment I was going to be sick. Not that I hadn't known all along that the time would come when Ralph would go, but I had never let myself think about it. Now, suddenly, I did think about it, and I didn't see how I would be able to bear it.

"I'll miss you!" I said. "Oh, Ralph, I do love you!" The words came tumbling out of their own accord, and I didn't have to plan them at all.

It was a long while before we rejoined Vietti and Anna on the front porch. When we did, we found they had the porch lights on and he was sitting on the arm of her chair, showing her something. As we came up the steps, he quickly thrust it into his pocket and stood up.

"We'd better get going," he said, "if we're going to catch the bus back to camp."

Ralph said, "I guess so." He gave me a long look. "Tomorrow night, Janie?"

I said, "Yes."

Vietti hesitated and then asked, "Would it be okay if we went along with you?"

Ralph didn't like the idea much, but there wasn't anything he could do about it. "Sure," he said. "I guess so."

Anna and I waited until the boys had set off at a half run toward and corner, and then we went into the house. We didn't talk much as we undressed for bed. We were both too busy with our own thoughts. When we finally turned out the light, I lay quiet in the darkness, seeing Ralph's face and hearing his voice say, "I love you," and feeling the empty ache deep inside me that came with the realization that soon—much, much too soon—he would be gone.

"Janie?" Anna said at last. "Are you awake?"

"Yes." I felt suddenly guilty about not having shown

any interest in Anna's evening. "Did you have a good time tonight?"

"Oh, yes," Anna said softly. "He's wonderful, Janie. But back in Chicago, he has a girl, a serious one I think."

"How do you know?" I asked.

"He told me, and then he showed me her picture. She's not very pretty, but she looks nice. She signed the picture, 'All my love, Clara.' He says she's the only girl he's ever gone steady with."

"Well," I said impatiently, "since when do you have to worry about other girls? She's there, and you're here. And you looked so pretty tonight."

"I felt pretty," Anna said softly.

She stopped talking then, and I let my mind go back to Ralph. I thought about him until I went to sleep.

We doubled often after that, never going anywhere especially exciting, but always having fun. I couldn't understand why Vietti had not wanted to date Anna in the first place, for it seemed to me that they had more fun together than any two people I had ever known. They laughed a lot and they talked easily, and sometimes they would just sit quietly, not touching each other, not having to talk. I had seen Anna date many boys and she had always seemed to have a good time, but I had never seen her like this. There was a glow about her now, a sense of contentment, and there was the same thing about him. It was as though they belonged together. It was the kind of feeling Ralph and I had—almost—but not quite.

"Admit you were wrong about Anna and Vietti," I said to Ralph teasingly. "Did you ever see a more perfect couple in your life?"

He shook his head stubbornly. "I don't know. He's got a girl back home."

"She's a part of his past," I said. "They're not cemented with Super Glue."

Ralph seemed doubtful. "Something's off about this, Janie. Other guys come back to the barracks at night and talk about their girlfriends, where they went and what they did and all. I know I sure do. Vietti never says a word about Anna. Most of the guys don't even know he's dating her. It's like he's ashamed of it or something."

"I don't believe it," I said. And, I didn't, really. But from then on, whenever I saw Anna, I immediately thought of what Ralph had said, and it kept on making me uncomfortable.

Anna, though, had never seemed happier.

"Oh, Janie," she whispered in class one morning, under cover of her English book, "I believe he's forgotten about her."

"Who?"

"Clara, of course. That girl in Chicago. He never talks about her anymore."

I hesitated and then whispered back, "Are you sure?"

Her eyes were warm, and her face was bright with happiness.

"I think—in fact, I almost know—he's in love with me."

"How?" I whispered. "How do you know?"

"I can't tell you exactly. It's just—oh, you can feel it when somebody loves you. You just know it, that's all."

Indeed I did know. Because now, the closer we drew to the day of the boys' transfer, the surer I became that Ralph loved me. It wasn't just his saying so; it was the way he kept his arm possessively around me whenever we talked to other boys and the way his voice got shaky when he mentioned leaving.

"I don't want to go," he said miserably one evening. "Blast it, Janie, I don't want to go!"

I said, "I'll be here when you get back, Ralph."

He started to draw me toward him, and I wondered suddenly what had become of the fun we used to have on our dates. It seemed to me now that all the time we had together was spent clinging to each other, agonizing about the years we would be apart.

I was just going to try to put this into words when Ralph said, "Let's get married."

"What!"

"Let's get married, Janie," he whispered. "Please! Then I'll know you're mine for keeps. You'll belong to me, and when I get back you'll be here. It'll give me something to hang onto, knowing that."

"Get married!" I repeated. Of course, I wanted to be married, someday. But that day had always seemed so far away, somewhere in a distant future. Never now. The idea of getting married now was overwhelming.

"You do love me," Ralph insisted, "don't you?"

"Yes," I said. "But, *married!* Why, I couldn't—"

"Please," Ralph said again. And then he said, "Janie, I need you."

Why, I thought in bewilderment, he's afraid! I looked up at him, and his face was a familiar, beloved blur in the darkness. I wished there was a moon so I could see it clearly, although I knew it by heart—the way his hair curled sideways in front of the silly little Air Force cap, the freckles across his nose, the way one eyebrow went up when he talk-ed. It wasn't a handsome face, but it was Ralph, and he was young and scared and was going to face a dangerous world he wasn't ready for, and he needed me.

"Yes," I said. "I'll marry you."

He kissed me then, and I thought, *Now I'm engaged. This is my first engaged kiss. A minute ago I was just a girl out on a date, and now I am engaged.*

I couldn't quite believe it.

When Ralph started to release me, I clung to him a little longer than usual, smelling the good, clean smell of soap and shaving lotion, feeling his nearness through the stiffness of his uniform. Then he boosted himself up and sat beside me on the porch railing, keeping his arm around me. We were very close and happy and there didn't seem to be much to say.

After a while Ralph asked, "Do you want the wedding here?"

"Why, of course," I said. "Where else would we have it?"

"Here is fine with me," Ralph said. "I'll have a few days' leave before I have to report in at my next base, and we can use that for a honeymoon."

I caught my breath.

"You mean, right away?" I could imagine Mother's and Daddy's faces if I walked into the house and announced, "I'm getting married next week."

"My parents wouldn't ever say yes to anything like that," I said. "They'll want all the formalities—an engage-ment and meeting your folks and having a nice wedding and everything. In fact," I finished lamely, "they'll probably not want us to get married at all. They've been planning for me to go to college."

"We can always elope," Ralph said, giving me a quick hug. He said it so casually that it took me a moment to realize that he was serious.

"No," I said. "I don't want to do it that way. I'll tell my folks about it. I'll explain how it is with you going overseas soon. They'll understand; they're pretty swell about understanding things."

But I was relieved to find Mother's and Daddy's bedroom door closed when I went in that night. I hesitated a moment and then went on to my room.

"I'll tell them in the morning," I told myself, "after I've talked it over with Anna. She'll help me think of the best way to tell them."

I didn't have a chance, however, because the next morning it was Anna who came to me.

"He hasn't called," she told me miserably. "Not in one whole week."

"You mean Vietti?" I was so surprised that I actually forgot my own problem for an instant. "I thought you two were crazy about each other!"

"We were," Anna said. "I don't know what happened, Janie. We didn't have a fight or anything. It was all just wonderful. In fact, it was *more* than wonderful. On the next-to-last night I saw him—" Her voice trailed off.

"Go on," I prodded impatiently. "What happened on the next-to-last night you saw him?"

"He kissed me," Anna said softly.

"Of course, he kissed you. Doesn't he always? You've been going together for months now. Don't tell me he'd never kissed you up until then?"

"A peck goodnight at the end of a date, but we'd never made out," Anna said. "I was even starting to worry that he might be one of those guys who have friendships with girls but don't get physically attracted to them. But the next-to-last night I saw him, it was like everything in him exploded, and he grabbed me and started kissing me like he never wanted to stop. He told me that he adores me—that he dreams about me every night—that I'm the most wonderful thing that has ever entered his life.

"The next night he came over for dinner, and I haven't heard from him since. It's like he's disappeared off the face of the earth."

"Could your folks have said something to hurt his feelings?" I asked. "Maybe he got the impression they didn't approve of him."

"Oh, no," Anna said at once. "You know Mom and Dad. They make everybody feel at home. He knew they liked him; why, when he left, Mom even said something about his being sure to come to dinner more often because she was glad I was going with such a nice boy. They couldn't have been any nicer to him."

"Perhaps he's sick and in the infirmary," I suggested. "Or was transferred suddenly to another base without having a chance to tell you."

She regarded me almost hopefully.

"Do you think that's possible?"

"Certainly," I assured her. "You never can tell with the Air Force."

"But wouldn't Ralph have told you?"

"Not necessarily," I said. Ralph and I were too deeply

concerned with our own relationship these days to worry about anyone else's. "I'll ask him about it tonight."

But I didn't have a chance because Ralph was in an irritable mood, and we spent the evening arguing because I hadn't yet told my parents about our decision to get married.

Anna didn't mention Vietti again. She came to school the next day looking as pretty as ever, and her assignments were as perfect as ever, and she was as pleasant and friendly with everyone as she had ever been. I found myself wondering if she were really as much in love with Vietti as I had thought, but then I remembered her face the morning she had whispered, "I think—he's in love with me!" and I was ashamed of my doubts.

That evening, when Ralph came by to take me to an early movie, I asked him immediately, before he had time to bring up the other subject at all.

He looked at me oddly.

"What's the matter? Do you miss him?"

"Don't be silly," I said. "I'm just asking because of Anna. She likes him, you know, an awful lot."

"You're sure," said Ralph, "that it's not you who likes him?"

In the beginning I had been flattered by Ralph's jealousy—it had made me feel important—but now it was beginning to irritate me. I found myself wondering if it was something he would outgrow when he was older and more sure of himself or if it was a trait that was going to hang on forever. I began to wish I knew.

"No," I said decidedly, "it's not me—it's Anna. She's worried sick about Vietti, and I told her I'd ask you about him."

I don't know what Ralph was going to answer because at that precise moment I glanced across the street and saw Vietti himself going into Jack's Tavern.

Jack's had a pretty fair reputation, and most of the Air Force boys went there. I had never been inside, but I had heard that it was decorated with Chinese lanterns and had a dance floor and wasn't really too bad a place. Daddy had asked me not to go there, and so I didn't, but I wasn't astonished to see Vietti there. What did surprise me was that it was only seven o'clock on a Tuesday evening, and I didn't think anybody ever went to such places at that hour.

Ralph followed my gaze.

"Well," he said, "that answers your question. He's still around all right. I guess he's just lost interest in Anna."

"No," I said. "I don't believe it."

I had seen Anna and Vietti together too often to believe that. They were too perfect for each other for one of them just to get tired of the other.

I turned abruptly and started back along the street the way we had come.

"Hey," said Ralph. "Where do you think you're going?" He whirled and caught up at me. "I thought we were going to the show!"

I said, "I'm going to get Anna."

Ralph caught my arm. "Janie, are you crazy?"

"Anna wants to talk to Vietti," I said, "and here's her chance. He'll be leaving here soon, and if she doesn't talk to him now she'll never know what went wrong between them and she'll always worry about it. We'll get her now and bring her over and give them a chance to patch things up."

Ralph was still arguing about it when we reached Anna's house. She was sitting in the living room doing her homework when we arrived. She didn't say one word when I told her. She just went to the closet and got her jacket and called to her mother, who was upstairs, that she was going out for half an hour with Ralph and me.

"I guess you believe I don't have much pride," she said once to Ralph on our way over. "Well, you're right. I don't."

She spoke quietly and, to my surprise, Ralph reached over and patted her arm.

"Sure," he said in a surprisingly gentle voice. "I guess you've got a right to know." And for the first time I began to wonder if Ralph might have guessed at something that I had not.

Vietti was sitting alone in a booth in the corner. He had a beer in front of him, but he didn't seem to be drinking it, he was just sitting there. He saw us immediately when we came in, but he didn't move. He lifted his eyes and stared at Anna, and as we crossed the room he still sat staring at her, as though he couldn't tear his eyes away.

"Hello," Ralph said awkwardly. "Can we join you?"

"Sure," Vietti said. He slid over and Anna sat down beside him, and Ralph and I slipped into the seats across from them. A waitress came over and asked us what we wanted to drink. Ralph ordered a beer for himself and Cokes for Anna and me, and the girl disappeared again.

"Well," said Vietti after a moment, "I never expected to see you girls in here. Your folks wouldn't like it much."

"No," Anna said. "I don't suppose they would." She was looking at him directly, without being coy or subtle. "I've missed you," she said.

"I've missed you too," Vietti said. "A lot."

"Ralph and Janie brought me here," Anna continued, "because I had to see you and find out what's gone wrong. I've gone with a lot of boys, but I've never felt about any of them the way I do about you. And I thought—I was sure—especially after that one special night, that you felt the same way about me. I don't know what happened. I need to know."

Her voice shook a little, and Ralph and I squirmed uncomfortably, feeling as though we had no right to be in on this conversation. But we were, and there was no getting out of it.

"That special night should never have happened," said Vietti. "I don't know what got into me. Can't we forget about it?"

He looked at her, and then he answered himself.

"No, I guess we can't. It was actually the next night when we spent the evening with your folks, that I realized how wrong it all was. They were so swell to me, with your mom inviting me back and saying how glad she was that I was going out with you. I knew then that I couldn't go on seeing you—not with Clara."

"Clara!" Anna looked surprised. "Why, I thought you'd almost forgotten Clara!"

"That's just it," Vietti said. "I had." He took a deep breath. "Clara—she isn't just an old girlfriend. Clara's my *wife.*"

We all just sat in stunned silence, unable to believe we had heard him correctly.

"Your wife!" I exclaimed at last. "You mean—"

"We were married," Vietti continued miserably, "when

we found out I was going to be drafted. We'd been dating for a couple of months, and we thought we were in love. I was going away. We were scared of losing each other, and so we eloped. We had three days together before I left.

"Anna," and now he was talking only to Anna, as though he had forgotten that Ralph and I were there, "I never meant for anything like this to happen. When I went out with you that first time, it was because I was so darned lonely. I didn't think it would do any harm just to go with a crowd again. I never imagined how it would be with us. Clara was the first girl I ever went steady with. I never thought—Anna, I can't believe I'm married! We only had three days together. Except for her picture, I can hardly remember what Clara looks like. I close my eyes and try, and all I can see on the back of my eyelids is you!"

To my horror I realized that he was crying. I knew I should be disgusted, but I wasn't. I just sat there watching him, thinking how very young he was and how unready for anything like this. I felt desperately sorry for him—and for Anna—and mostly, perhaps, for Clara. I had never met Clara, and yet I felt as though I knew her best of all.

Ralph reached over and took my hand.

"Come on, Janie," he said. "I'd better get you home."

Anna said, "I'll come too." She got up with us.

Ralph hesitated. "You don't want to stay—to discuss things?"

"No," Anna said.

We didn't talk on the way back to my house after we dropped Anna off at her place. We just walked along the dark streets, holding hands, listening to the click of our footsteps on the pavement. I was trying to think how to tell

Ralph what I had to tell him.

I don't want a hurry-up marriage! I thought. *I want time. Time to finish growing up and see what kind of people we are going to turn into. Time for planning. Time to live together and build a good sound marriage, not three days that can be forgotten as soon as we are apart. I don't want to be Clara!*

Out loud I said, "I don't want to be Clara, Ralph!"

He didn't ask me to explain. He just said, "No, honey. And I don't want you to be."

After the boys' training ended, Ralph had a couple of days' leave which he spent in Trenton with his family, and then he went to some base in California. I got a letter from him written there, and then it was over a month before I heard from him again. That time Ralph's letter was mailed from Germany.

It's hard to tell much about people in letters; they can change a lot in three years. Anna's pinned now to Don, a boy from Carolina State—a nice boy—I guess they'll get married after they graduate. So there wasn't any heartbroken tremor in her voice when she said, "I wonder what he hears from Vietti." Not any more. She just wonders.

I wonder too, of course. And I wonder about Ralph—how he has changed—what it will be like between us when we do see each other again.

Oh, well, he'll soon be back in the States, and he says he'll be down to see me. Then, I guess, we'll know. Or, if we don't know, we'll have time to find out.

(written at the age of 18)

☆ ☆ ☆ ☆ ☆ ☆ ☆ ☆ ☆ ☆ ☆ ☆ ☆ ☆

"Time To Find Out" portrays a situation that was common in the early fifties when boys in their teens were being drafted straight out of high school and sent to military training bases all over the country. They were often away from home for the first time in their lives and were lonely and lost and desperate for companionship.

One of those training camps was in my home town of Sarasota. High school girls (usually seniors) were thrilled to date those young men who looked so exotically handsome in their uniforms. I was one of those girls, and another was my good friend, Anna.

I dated Ralph, and Anna dated Vietti. Beyond those two facts, this particular story is fiction. But it accurately portrays the situation that was faced by numerous young people, caught up in the frenzy of brief, intense wartime romances that didn't have time to mature before the men/boys were sent off to possibly die on some distant battlefield. Those romances resulted in a rash of hasty and unwise young marriages in an era when divorce was almost unheard of.

When I was trying to locate a copy of this story to include in this anthology, Anna supplied it. She had kept it in her scrapbook all these years. She's never forgotten Vietti.

The Lost Christmas

"Rick, will you give me a ride uptown?"

"Nope. I'm busy."

"Then may I use your car? It won't take long; I just have to pick up my new dress."

"Are you crazy? You know I never lend my car to anybody." Rick glanced up from the paper on which he was scribbling. "I'm totally up all my expenses for New Year's Eve—tickets, corsage, and dinner at a really nice restaurant. I hope Midge isn't a big eater."

"From what I hear, she's the type to order pheasant under glass." I tried to sound beguiling. "Please, Rick—the snow has turned to slush, and I don't want to have to hike to the bus and back. It's Christmas Eve—why not show a little brotherly love?"

Rick sighed and laid the paper aside. "It doesn't feel much like Christmas this year. As far as I'm concerned, it's kind of turned into nothing. Maybe we've outgrown it or something."

"No," I said. "It's not that. It's that Mother isn't here."

I don't think any of us had realized before how important Mother's warmth and enthusiasm were in binding our family together—not until this year when she was spending the holidays with her parents because Grandma was ill. Suddenly it was as though there was no Christmas at all. Dad had taken Mother to our grandparents' house—a two hour drive each way—and returned to immerse himself in affairs at his office.

At home on our own, Rick and I had little to say to each other.

Mother had now been gone for almost a week, and I had been too occupied with the unaccustomed extra duties of cooking and housekeeping to think much about the coming holiday. Dad had bought a tree—a lopsided little fir, because the good ones had been picked over by the time he reached the tree lot—and I had decorated it. It sat now in the corner of the living room, overloaded with ornaments and already beginning to shed its needles.

"At least there's the dance," I said "That should be fun, and I have to get my dress. It's my one big Christmas present from Mother and Dad, the way the seat belts in your car were for you. The shop had to order it specially from its New York store because they didn't have a blue one in stock, and they phoned this morning to say it has come. Please, Rick—the store's going to be closed all Christmas week and I have to have my new formal for New Year's Eve!"

"Oh, all right," Rick said ungraciously. "Sometimes I envy guys who don't have sisters. At least, they don't have to act as private taxi services."

He stood up, holding himself very straight, trying to stretch a couple of extra inches onto his height. Although Rick is a senior, he is only two inches taller than I am. But he's nice-looking, with curly hair and very blue eyes and a nice smile—when he smiles.

He was not smiling now. "Come on," he said, and we went into the hall to put on our coats and then out through the kitchen to the garage.

We have a double garage. On one side, Dad keeps his station wagon, and Rick has taken the other for his car. Rick started saving for that car when he was twelve years old and our grandfather gave him five dollars for his birthday.

"I'm putting it in the bank," he announced immediately, "to save toward my car." And the very next day he had Dad go with him while he opened a savings account. From then on, half of his allowance and every extra dollar he earned at summer jobs went into his car fund. The week after he turned sixteen he bought the car.

"It's secondhand, of course," he said, "but it's in great condition. Take a look at that engine!"

He raised the hood to display the car's inner workings—wires and hoses and little black plugs with grease on them. I think we all were amazed that he knew so much about what went on inside an engine.

Mother said, "That's wonderful, dear—just wonderful," but later, after Rick had left to take the car to show off to his friends, she had asked Dad, "Do you think we should let him have it? He seems so terribly young still," and Dad had responded, "There's not much we can do about it. He paid for the thing himself, you know."

So the car moved into the garage next to Dad's, and Dad said sometimes that he was ashamed to see them there together, because Rick's was always so brightly polished.

Now, however, as we walked over to it, I had the funny feeling that the car, like the little Christmas tree, was a trifle lopsided.

I asked, "What's the matter with it?"

"The matter?" Rick had been opening the garage door, and now he turned in alarm. "What do you mean?"

"It sits lower on one side than on the other."

"You're crazy," Rick said. "It couldn't—" And then he stopped. In a few quick steps he reached the far side of the car. "Oh, no! The tire's flat! It's not only flat, it's finished. It's slashed right through the sidewall! It must have hit against a rock or something!"

"Oh, dear!" I glanced at my watch. "How long will it take you to change it?"

There was a moment's silence. When Rick spoke again there was an odd note in his voice. "I can't change it."

"Why not? You have a jack, don't you? Why can't you just put on the spare?"

"I don't have a spare. Not any more." He stood gazing down at the deflated tire. "I sold my spare to Scotty Nolan."

"You sold it!"

"Yes. I had spent all my cash on Christmas presents, and then Midge said she'd go with me to the New Year's formal. I never thought she'd do it. And I had to have money for the ticket and the corsage—" His voice faded off.

"So you've been driving without a spare for weeks now!" I exclaimed reprovingly. "When Dad finds out he'll have a fit!"

"Well, go ahead and tell him, Miss Tattleblabber. That's the least of my worries. This finishes off my date with Midge for New Year's. Even if you don't tell him, Dad's bound to notice, and you know he won't advance me the money to replace it. He'll say I got what I deserved and this should be a lesson."

"You won't have to miss the dance," I said. "You can always ride with Dave and me. Dave's uncle is going to drive us and pick us up afterward."

"Thanks, but no thanks," Rick said shortly.

"Why? Are you so embarrassed by your kid sister that you don't want your precious Midge to be exposed to her?"

"Oh, come off it, Connie. It's not anything like that, and you know it. It's just that—that—" His voice was low and shaky.

Suddenly to my surprise the toughness was gone from his face; it looked young and vulnerable, the way it had a long time ago when we were children. "How do you suppose I got a date with Midge in the first place? Do you really think a girl as popular as she is would date a shrimp like me when she could be going with any one of a dozen taller guys? It's the car that did it. I'm one of the few seniors who has his own car to take her in."

"For goodness sake, Rick!" I said, "Why do you want to date her if she's like that?"

"Because she's—she's—" His face was bright red. "Well, why do you like Dave so much? He's not all all that perfect as far as I can see, but you can't help it, you just want to go out with him. That's how I feel about Midge. I thought maybe if she went out with me a few times and got a chance to know me better, she might have fun—I mean she'd see that just being short doesn't mean a guy's not worth going out with, and then she'd like me for *me*—not just for the car." He was stumbling along miserably when he seemed to remember who he was talking to. He cleared his throat, and when he spoke again the old cockiness was back in his voice. "Oh, what's the difference? There'll be other dances.

You'd better get going if you want to make it to the bus stop."

The bus was just pulling up to the corner when I reached it. I ran the last few yards and stumbled up the steps into the warm interior. Dropping my change into the slot, I made my way to the back and sank into the only empty seat. Then I relaxed and leaned back to look about me. The bus was crowded with people laughing and talking, clutching bags and boxes and odd-shaped parcels. The woman in the next seat over had an armload of Christmas wreaths, and their piney odor drifted back to me in a wave of spicy sweetness. Behind me, two children, a boy and a girl, were giggling together over a package they had precariously balanced on the seat between them, and every few minutes one of them would peek inside to see that whatever it contained was still there.

Glancing back at them, I felt a wave of nostalgia, for they reminded me so much of Rick and me at their ages. We had been inseparable then, riding our bicycles and building club houses and sharing secrets.

"I'm glad my children are so close in age," Mother had said one time. "That makes them such wonderful companions. No matter what happens during their lives, they will always have each other to fall back on."

Remembering the words now, I was filled with an empty sense of loss. What, I asked myself in bewilderment, had happened? The friendship, the closeness, the fun and companionship we had shared, where had it gone? Somehow, during the past few years it had vanished. Rick had gone his way and I mine. With Mother at home, it had not been so noticeable; her love for both of us had seemed to draw the family together. But now, in her absence, the truth became apparent. Rick and I had found our separate friends, our separate interests; we were pulling apart in different directions. The brother I had once known so well had become to me almost a stranger—aloof and cocky and superior, irritated by and scornful of everything I did and said.

Almost a stranger, and yet *not quite*. I remembered his face as I had seen it in the garage—a face gone young with misery. There had been nothing superior about it then.

The bus had reached town now and was pulling up to the corner in front of the dress shop. I got up. The two children behind me were still giggling together as I started down the aisle to the door. Clutching my purse, I clambered down the steps to the sidewalk, knowing what I had to do.

The saleslady at the counter looked up with a smile as I came in. "Hello, there! Can I help you?"

"Yes," I said. "I want to return a dress."

"To return—" She glanced at my empty arms. "Don't you have it with you?"

"It's already here," I said. "You're holding it for Connie Parker. It's a formal ankle-length taffeta, like the pink one in the front window, only blue. My mother ordered it for me as a Christmas present."

"I see." The girl looked puzzled. "Then you've decided you don't want the dress after all?"

"That's right. Mother has already paid for it. I would like a refund instead."

"This is rather irregular. I'll have to speak to the manager. Will you wait a minute please?" The girl disappeared into a back room. When she returned a few moments later she was carrying a box with a slip of paper attached to it. "I can refund the money if you want, but it does seem a shame. The dress is lovely. Wouldn't you like to look at it before you decide?"

"No, thank you," I said. "I'll just take the money, please."

I forced my eyes away from the box. I knew perfectly well that it was a lovely dress. I knew what it would do for me too, the shimmering ice blue—that it would put blonde highlights into my hair and make my eyes larger and bluer. I had hoped that when Dave saw me in it I would seem different to him—not just a pleasant girl to take occasionally to dances but someone special. I had hoped ... but I had a party dress at home, several years old and a little bit weary, but perfectly wearable even on New Year's Eve.

"I'll just take the money," I said again, and when it was in my purse I left quickly.

At a garage two blocks away I bought the tire. I did not know a thing about tires, and I did not know exactly what to ask for.

"I don't know what size," I said after telling him the make of Rick's car. "But it's for a fifty-seven two-door hardtop."

"What kind of tire?" the man asked me. "Tube or tubeless?"

"I don't know." He might as well have been speaking a foreign language. "Is there a difference?"

"Yes," the man said patiently, "there's a difference. Since it's a fifty-seven, I think you'd better take the tube too."

"All right," I agreed.

He went to the back of the garage and returned with a tire and a small flat box. "Here you are," he said, glancing around. "Where do you want me to put it? Is somebody picking you up here?"

"No," I said, "I'm going on the bus."

"You can't do that, Miss," he said. "Not with the holiday crowds. They'll never let you on a bus with something this big."

"I guess you're right." I counted out the money, seeing to my relief that there were a few dollars remaining from the price of the dress. "I guess, maybe, I'd better take a taxi."

Rick was out in front, shoveling the driveway, when the cab pulled up in front of our house. Dropping the shovel, he came to the curb to meet me.

"Where the devil did you get that?" he demanded when he caught sight of the tire.

"At a garage," I said snappishly. "Where else?"

"But what are you doing with it?"

"Giving it to you." I rolled it to him. It wobbled lopsidedly across the snow and he put out his hand and caught it. He kept staring at it as though he didn't believe it was real.

"Go jack it on," I said, "or however you do it. It's your Christmas present."

Rick was silent a moment. Then he said, "I thought we agreed we weren't going to give presents to each other this year. We were going to use our money to get extra nice things for Mother and Grandma."

"So I broke the agreement," I said. "Can't a girl change her mind without your making a federal case of it?" I was so irritated that I felt like slapping him. "Now you can take your precious Midge to the dance in style. You might at least say thank you."

"Well, sure," Rick said gruffly. "Thanks." He opened his

mouth as though he were going to say something more and then he closed it again.

"You're welcome," I said and went past him into the house.

Standing in the hallway, taking off my coat and galoshes, my eyes blurred with the hot sting of tears. I blinked them back angrily, asking myself just what it was that I had expected. Did I think Rick was going to fall to his knees in gratitude? Did I expect him to throw his arms around me and hug me—Rick, who had stopped hugging Mother by the time he was twelve years old?

No, I answered myself honestly, what I had wanted was even more than that. I had hoped to be able to go back eight years with one great leap and have us friends again, close friends the way we used to be. But things did not work that way. You could not pull closed a gap between people with a tire and a tube—not when the people had grown as far apart as we had.

On Christmas Day, Dad drove us to our grandparents' house. Mother met us at the door, and Dad and Rick and I gave her her presents, watching her face light up with love and pleasure as she untied the ribbons. Dad had gotten her a beautiful housecoat and a new charm or her bracelet. Rick gave her earrings and perfume, and I had spent every cent of my gift money on a white and gold evening bag.

"It's beautiful!" Mother gasped when she saw it, and she kissed me. "Everything is beautiful! I am so lucky to have such a wonderful family!" And again I found my eyes filling with tears.

Grandma was better, Mother told us, but still very weak. Grandpa took us up to see her for a few moments.

She looked small and frail in the big bed, but her hair was beautifully dressed as usual and her smile was as sweet as ever.

Our own house, when we got home again, seemed cold and empty. Dad parked the car while Rick and I went inside ahead of him and turned on the lights. I stopped in the living room and looked at the lopsided little tree, drooping sadly under the weight of its ornaments, and wondered why I had bothered decorating it in the first place. Rick had said that we had outgrown Christmas, and I realized now that he was right. Christmas was gone, a part of the fun of childhood, and we could never bring it back again.

The electric cord hung limply down one side of the tree, and on impulse I reached down and plugged it in. The lights sprang on in an array of colors, and their soft glow revealed that beneath the tree there was a square flat package. I knelt down and picked it up. It had not been there that afternoon, I was certain. The card on it said, "Merry Christmas to Connie."

I stared at it in astonishment. Then slowly and carefully I began to remove the wrappings. The box itself was so light that I could not believe there was anything in it. When I lifted the top, I saw that my guess was not a bad one, for all that was inside was a sheet of white paper on which there was pasted part of a picture from a magazine. It had been torn through and showed only the front hood and bumper of a car.

"What in the world … ?"

"It's one third," Rick said. I raised my eyes, and he was standing there looking down at me. "One third interest in my car."

"You mean—" I could not believe what I was hearing.

"One third interest," he said again. "That means you

can use it a third of the time, for club meetings and to go uptown and things like that. Or just to ride around in."

"Why, Rick—" I said, "Rick—"

For one brief moment, looking into his eyes, I saw reflected there all the things that were in my own heart, the things that I had thought to keep so carefully hidden— the problems and worries and dreams and fears that make growing up so difficult for a girl—or for a boy. I saw something else there too, wedged down deep, beneath the layers and layers of protective covering—clear and bright and unmistakable—the look of love.

"Well, after all," he said, "you are my sister." He shifted in sudden embarrassment, and the old gruffness came back into his voice. "Of course, you'll have to pay for your share of the gas."

"Of course," I said.

In the soft glow of the tree lights, the room was filled with Christmas. It had been there all the time.

(written at the age of 22)

☆　☆　☆　☆　☆　☆　☆　☆　☆　☆　☆　☆　☆　☆

In some ways this story is dated. Today it's far from unusual for seniors in high school—girls as well as boys—to own cars. A few dollars will no longer cover the cost of a taxi ride. And seat belt aren't considered a luxury, they're a legal necessity.

But, as with most of the stories in this collection, the issues I addressed are those that transcend the years. Relationships between brothers and sisters. The meaning of Christmas. And the way our perceptions change when we leave childhood behind us.

The Last Night

Anne is asleep. She sleeps quietly, lying on her side with one hand under her pillow. Her hair is rolled tightly in pin curls. Tomorrow it will lie soft and curly over her shoulders, but tomorrow night I shall not see her, for she will be gone. I watch her sleeping tonight as I have done so many years before, warm and close and all around her; for I am a part of her, and she is a part of me.

I am Anne's room. I am light blue walls and blue curtains and a bureau on which sit a comb and brush, a pink stuffed elephant, a picture of Larry and a container of bobby pins. I am a bookshelf which is two shades of blue, because Kendal started painting it and never got around to finishing. I contain a battered copy of *Robin Hood*, several volumes of poetry by Edna St. Vincent Millay, *Gone with the Wind*, a stack of paperback novels, and a rhyming dictionary. I am a rug with a nail polish stain on it, a scarred old desk full of letters and diaries and scrapbooks, the folding alarm clock Anne's father gave her when she was graduated from high school, and the silver inkwell which she never uses but won in an essay contest.

I have changed since yesterday, for clothes have been taken from my closet and packed in the two suitcases which lie open in the middle of my floor, and a new dress of a kind Anne has never owned before hangs on the closet door. Anne will wear it tomorrow.

But for tonight she is still mine, and I watch her as she stirs and smiles in her sleep. I know what she is dreaming, for I have known her for a very long time …

Anne enters for the first time. She is a chubby little girl with braces on her teeth and tight brown braids, and she bounces when she walks. She wrinkles her nose because I am not as large as she wanted me to be.

"The walls must be blue," she says at once. "I want the walls painted blue."

"Mother won't let you," says Kendal, who stands in the doorway with his hands in his pockets. "She says we're going to leave the walls just the way they are."

"No," declares Anne. "They will be blue."

"Mother!" Kendal screams in his high, shrill, little-boy's voice. "Anne says her room's got to be blue!"

Their mother's voice comes wearily, answering from downstairs where she is hanging curtains in the dining room. "We'll have blue curtains and a rug, and some of the furniture will be blue."

"No," Anne says firmly. "The whole room. Everything in the whole room must be blue."

She walks over to my window and looks out into the yard.

"There's a swing!"

"Is there? Where?" Kendal flies to the window too and pushes in beside her. "Oh, I see. You can't ride that, Annie. You're too fat."

Anne gives him a slap, and Kendal screams, "Mother!" But when there is no answer, he says, "Let's go play."

Their footsteps clatter on the stairs, and a moment later I hear their voices out by the swing. Kendal is saying, "You see? I told you! You're too fat!"

I have another occupant now. He is a dog named Turvey. Turvey is supposed to be half Kendal's dog, but he much prefers Anne who feeds him and brushes him and lets him sleep at the foot of her bed. Anne is going to be a veterinarian when she grows up and run a boarding kennel for dogs.

Kendal comes in often and sits on the foot of Anne's bed and swings his feet while she tells him stories. The stories are always the same—full of dragons and giants and princes on horseback—but even so, Kendal often gets so excited that he bounces on the bed until the springs creak. Turvey always leaves when Kendal comes in.

I see their mother once or twice a day when she comes in to bring clean laundry and to hang up Anne's pajamas and straighten her bed. She thinks Anne is old enough to do these things herself. Anne means to, but she usually forgets.

I scarcely ever see Anne's father, because he works in a law office all day and comes home just in time for dinner, after which he sits in the living room with Anne's mother for a while and then goes to bed. Occasionally he will rap sharply on my door at night and say, "Daughter, it's time your light was off." Then Anne will say, "Yes, Daddy," and turn off her light for a few minutes and when he is safely gone she will turn it on again and pick up her book and start reading where she left off.

Turvey is not quite housebroken yet, but he is still only a puppy.

Anne is getting ready to go to a party. She is putting on lipstick in front of the mirror. Her hair is not in pigtails now; it is combed back from her face and held with a ribbon, and her dress is soft and fluffy and blue and swishes when she moves.

She steps back from the mirror and looks at herself.

"Mother!" she calls. "Mother, come look! I'm beautiful!"

Her mother comes in, and her face goes warm and soft.

"Darling," she says. "You will have a wonderful time."

"Of course," Anne agrees.

They go downstairs together and I hear Anne's father start the car in the driveway.

Her mother calls, "Be careful of your dress when you shut the car door."

The car leaves, and I wait.

Turvey comes in and jumps onto the bed. He lies on the pillow because he knows no one will come in and tell him to get down. There is a little pool of pink nail polish on the rug where Anne spilled it in the excitement of getting ready.

Time passes. The clock in the downstairs hall strikes eight and nine and ten and eleven. The lights go out in the house next door.

I hear the car in the driveway again. The door opens and closes.

Anne's father says, "You're sure I didn't come to get you too early? The other kids didn't seem ready to leave yet."

"No," Anne says.

Anne's mother calls from her room. "How was it, dear?"

"Fine, Mother."

"Come in and tell me about it."

"Some other time," Anne says. "I'm very sleepy."

Her mother's voice is disappointed. "All right, darling," she says. "Goodnight."

Anne opens my door, and she is not beautiful anymore. She is only a plump girl in a tight blue dress with too much lipstick on her mouth.

Turvey, looking guilty, gets off the pillow quickly and moves to the foot of the bed. Anne throws herself down beside him and buries her face against his back and begins to cry.

"Oh, Turvey," she sobs, "I'm *fat!*"

All at once, Turvey is dead. He was run over by a milk truck early this morning, and Anne's father found him in the road on his way to work.

Anne does not own a black dress, but she ties a black ribbon in her hair.

Kendal is crying very loudly.

"He was half mine," he sobs.

"No," Anne says. "He was not yours at all. He was all mine because he loved me the best."

"He didn't!" Kendal wails. "He didn't! He didn't!"

Suddenly Anne goes to him and puts her arm around him.

"No," she said quietly, "of course he didn't. He was *our* dog and he loved us both the same."

They bury Turvey in the yard out behind the swing.

This summer I do not see much of Anne. She blows in and out, very tall and tan in her white tennis shorts and bright-colored halters. Her braces are gone now and she wears only a retainer at night after she goes to bed. Although her mother has taken in all her clothes, they still seem to be baggy around the waist.

When I do see her she is usually with another girl and they are talking and giggling. Someone named Jed has given Anne a pink stuffed elephant, and Anne and the other girl laugh a lot at that.

"Oh, what a romantic thing to give a girl! An elephant!"

"What on earth did you say when he gave it to you?"

"Say? Why, I said, 'Oh, Jed, every time I look at this it will remind me of you.'"

"Anne, you didn't!"

"Of course, I didn't, silly. I said 'How cute.' What else could I say?"

The telephone rings a lot. Although it is located in a different part of the house, Anne now has become so much a part of me that I sometimes can follow her energy to other rooms. Never beyond the door that leads to the outside, but certainly as far as the telephone, since Anne is on it so much that it's become an appendage.

"Anne, it's for you!"

"Who is it?"

"I don't know!" Kendal shouts deliberately into the receiver. "It could be any of them. You've got so many, I can't keep them straight!"

Kendal, too, has changed. He is taller than Anne now and his treble has dropped to an uncertain rumble that breaks occasionally into a surprised squeak.

He waits while Anne talks. Suddenly his grin fades and he looks worried.

"Annie," he says when she hangs up, "you don't ever let those guys kiss you, do you?"

Anne looks surprised.

"Some of them," she says. "Once in a while."

"Which ones?"

"Only Peter and Jed. And only sometimes."

"Well, I don't think it's right," Kendal says sternly. "I don't think you should let any boy kiss you unless you're really in love with him. Girls who do that have mean things said about them."

Their father comes in on the end of this.

"Hello," he says. "What's the conversation about?"

"Nothing," says Anne.

"Nothing," says Kendal.

They smile at each other, and their father is awkward and out of it all, very much apart. He shrugs his shoulders, turns away, and picks up the evening paper.

Anne is writing an essay. She writes slowly, breathing hard, leaning forward over her desk.

At first she writes with difficulty, but then suddenly the words start to come. They begin to fall into a pattern, to say what she wants them to say. Her pen races across the page and the lovely words pour onto the paper, swiftly, easily, beautifully; and she writes faster and faster in a glow of wonder.

Kendal comes to the door.

"Dinner, Annie."

"Go away."

"Aren't you hungry?"

"No."

He leaves and a few minutes later her mother appears.

"Is anything wrong, Anne? Are you sick?"

"No. I'm busy."

Her mother says firmly, "Come to dinner this minute before everything gets cold."

Anne sits at the dinner table without speaking, eating nothing, trying to keep the spell from breaking.

Her father says, "What's the matter, daughter?"

"Nothing."

"She's writing something," says her mother.

"An essay," Anne says. "For a school contest."

"How nice."

They finish dinner and Anne comes again to her desk and reaches for the words. They are still there, shining and golden at her mind's edge. They tremble on her pen and dance onto the paper. She finishes one page and lays it aside and begins another and finishes that and begins another. Her pen runs out of ink. She fills it again and writes on.

At last she is done. She picks up the papers and goes into the hall.

"Mother!" she calls, but to her amazement the house is dark and silent. She looks at the hall clock and it is a quarter to three.

She goes to her parents' bedroom door.

"Mother," she calls softly, "I've finished the essay!"

"Fine, dear. I hope you win." Her mother's voice is thick with sleep.

"Mother, it's good. It's very good. I can tell." Her voice is leaping with excitement. "Mother, I know what I am going to do! I'm going to become a writer!"

But her mother is fast asleep.

She comes to me again and lays the pages on the desk.

"Goodness," she says, "I'm hungry!" She smiles happily.

It is a hot day. The gown is long and white and woolen. Anne hates wearing it because the heat makes it itch, but there is nothing she can do about it.

"At least, let me wear the cap back on my head," she says snappishly as her mother pushes it forward.

"Anne, it's not *supposed* to go on the back. It's supposed to sit perfectly flat on top."

"But then I don't have any hair sticking out at all. I look like an egg."

Kendal comes in. He grins.

"Well, look at that! The sweet girl graduate in person!"

Her father comes to the door. He stands there for a long moment, not saying anything. He is looking for a child, but there is no child to see. There is a tall, young woman in a cap and gown who smiles at him as though she knows him very well, but he does not remember ever having seen her before.

He says, "Daughter, I have something for you, a little present." He holds out the alarm clock. It is little and silver and lovely it its leather case. The case is blue.

Anne cries, "Daddy! Oh, Daddy!"

She had not expected an alarm clock, but now that she has one she knows she could never live without it.

She runs to him, and he knows her again now. Her mother and Kendal gather to examine the present. They are all close together, warm and laughing, the four of them; and their laughter flows through me until I am warm and very full.

I am waiting. I am still Anne's room. I am still full of Anne's things, but Anne is absent. She writes often from college, but her letters are usually read in other parts of the house. I cannot extend to those parts without Anne's presence in them, so all I know of the letters is from scattered remarks I hear as people pass by my doorway.

"I'm glad she likes her roommate." "I hope she won't start smoking." "Larry Chockworth. Odd name—Chockworth. She says he's very nice. But then she used to say that Jed was nice too." "How much did she say that sorority would cost?"

I am waiting. I am still Anne's room, but I am not complete until Anne is here.

Anne comes home for Christmas vacation. She is glad to be home, and she hugs her family and hangs tinsel on the tree and goes skating with Kendal and his girlfriend and teases her father and laughs with her mother; but she is different. She is no longer theirs. Her mind is full of things they do not even suspect.

"Mother," Anne says, "I'm not so sure now about being a writer."

"Why, darling? I thought you had definitely decided."

"I don't know now. So many people are better than I am. Sometimes I think it would be better to let other people write the books and just be one of the people who reads them."

"Well, it's up to you, dear."

After a moment Anne says, "I think you would like Larry. The boy I wrote you about."

Then she laughs and begins to talk about other things she talks about so many things that when she leaves her family is not quite sure which were the important ones or if any of them were important at all.

Kendal is painting the bookshelf as a surprise for Anne when she comes home for spring vacation. He has it only half done, because the paint is too thick and he has to keep thinning it with turpentine.

His mother comes in.

"Kenny," she says quietly, "you won't have to hurry with that shelf. I just got a letter from Anne, and she won't be home for spring vacation. She's been invited to spend the two weeks at Larry's home in North Carolina."

Kendal dangles the wet paint brush in one hand.

"You're not going to *let* her?"

"Yes," says his mother. "If that's how she wants to spend her vacation, I want her to do it."

"But she ought to come home. She can see him all year long at college."

His mother sighs, and he puts his arm around her awkwardly.

"Gee whiz, Mother," he says. "I'm still here."

His voice is deep now like his father's, and his shoulders are broad, and his long face crinkles up when he smiles.

His mother says, "Oh, Kenny, I'm so glad I have a daughter *and* a son!"

Anne has come home again, but she is not alone. She has brought a boy with her. He is a slender, quiet boy with blue eyes and a shy smile. Her father likes him. Kendal likes him too, despite himself, for he was all set to dislike him intensely. Anne's mother is not sure whether she likes him or not.

I see very little of Anne now. She comes in late at night and undresses slowly and goes to bed. Her body is slender and strong and lovely, but she does not know this yet. Sometimes she stands in front of the mirror and says, "Oh dear, I am too thin!" in just the way she used to croon, "I am too fat!"

"Oh," she whispers, "I want so much to be beautiful!"

She need not worry. In the eyes of the boy who sleeps in the guest room down the hall, she is, indeed, beautiful.

It is the last night before they return to college. It is not really night at all, but early morning. Anne comes in quietly and closes the door. Her face is soft with wonder and her eyes are shining. She stands alone in the middle of my floor and looks at the ring. The diamond burns and glows and fills me with its splendor, although it is only a tiny diamond.

"Oh," she whispers, "I love you! I love you!" and her voice leaps and sings, and she is half crying and half laughing at herself for being silly enough to cry, and she is too happy to care.

I draw about her and hold her close, because I know that soon she will be mine no longer. Soon she will be gone...

Anne is asleep. She stirs and smiles, for she is dreaming.

She has forgotten a broken swing and a dog named Turvey and a fat little girl in a too-tight party dress. But she will remember them again; for they are part of her, just a she is part of me.

I wait.

Before long the sky glows pink and the room begins to grow light. A milk truck rumbles down the street outside. A dog barks to be let out. Somewhere a baby cries.

Sunlight steals in the window. It rambles idly across the half-filled suitcases on the floor and beams on the creamy satin wedding dress where it hangs on the closet door. Then it climbs to the bed and tumbles carelessly across Anne's face.

She stretches and yawns and opens her eyes.

"Oh," she says joyfully, "what a lovely day!"

(written at the age of 18)

☆ ☆ ☆ ☆ ☆ ☆ ☆ ☆ ☆ ☆ ☆ ☆ ☆ ☆

This is my own story, written days before my wedding. I was "Anne." My brother was "Kendal."

"Turvey" was my first dog, Ginger.

The books on Anne's shelves were my favorite books.

The room was my room.

Writing this story was my way of saying goodbye to my childhood self and acknowledging how much this first chapter of my life had meant to me.

Other Titles You Will Enjoy
From Lizzie Skurnick Books

TO ALL MY FANS, WITH LOVE, FROM SYLVIE by Ellen Conford. Ellen Conford's classic 1982 road novel takes place over the course of five days as we follow the comic misadventures of fifteen-year-old Sylvie.

SECRET LIVES by Berthe Amoss. Set against the backdrop of 1930s New Orleans, Berthe Amoss's 1979 young adult mystery follows twelve-year-old Addie Agnew as she struggles to uncover the secret of her mother's death.

HAPPY ENDINGS ARE ALL ALIKE by Sandra Scoppetone. At a time when girls were only allowed to date boys, Jaret and Peggy know they had to keep their love a secret.

I'LL LOVE YOU WHEN YOU'RE MORE LIKE ME by M.E. Kerr. M.E. Kerr's beloved 1977 young adult classic tells the story of two very different teenagers, both struggling to stand up to their parents.

DEBUTANTE HILL by Lois Duncan. Lois Duncan's 1958 young adult classic tells the story of what happens when the debutante tradition comes to one small town.

Subscribe to Lizzie Skurnick Books and receive a book a month delivered right to your front door. Online at **http://igpub.com/lizzie-skurnick-books-subscription/**